P9-DXT-450

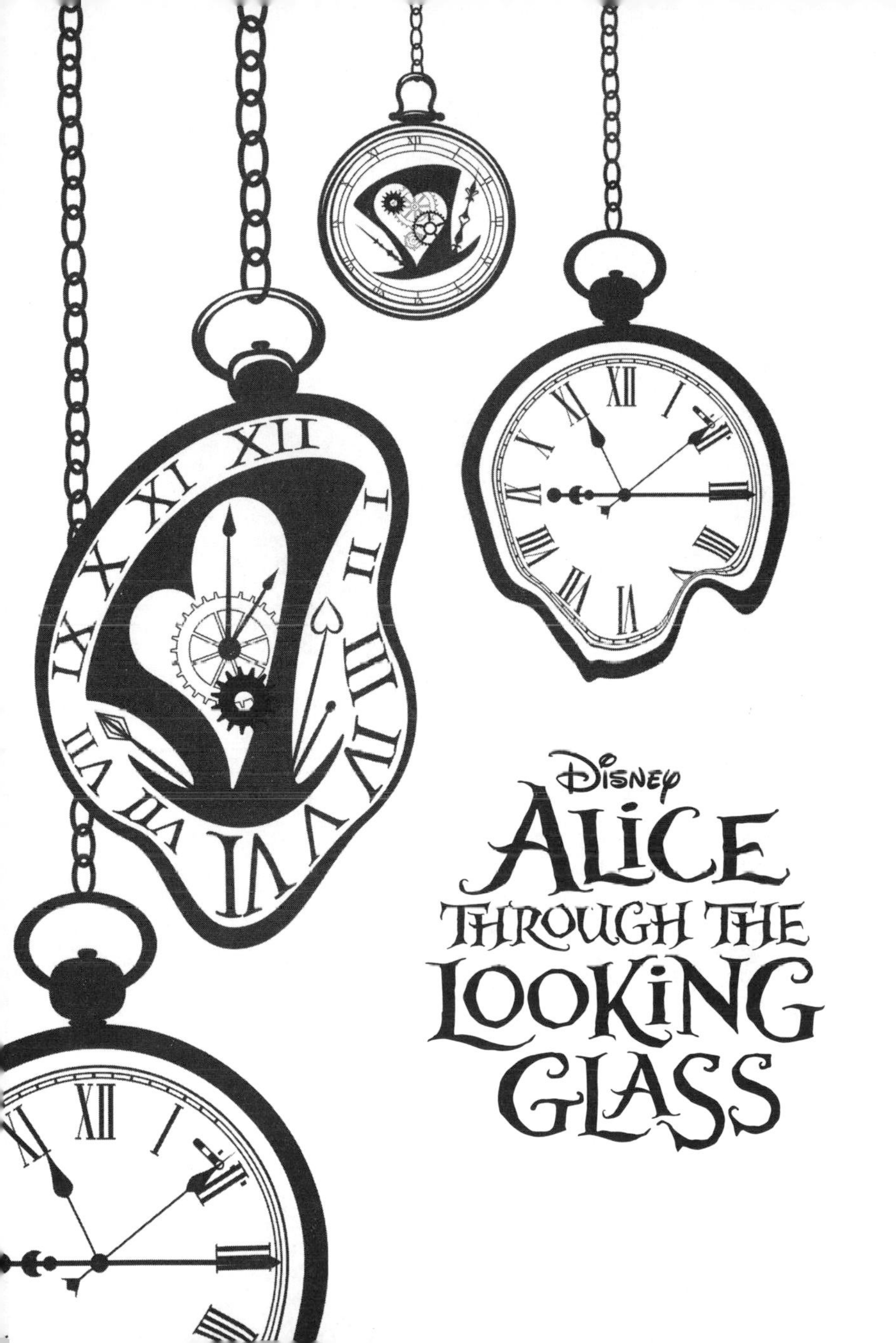
Disney
ALICE
THROUGH THE
LOOKING
GLASS

Adapted by
KARI SUTHERLAND

Based on the screenplay by
LINDA WOOLVERTON

Based on characters created by
LEWIS CARROLL

Produced by
JOE ROTH, SUZANNE TODD & JENNIFER TODD, TIM BURTON

Directed by
JAMES BOBIN

Disney PRESS
Los Angeles • New York

Printed in the United States of America
First Hardcover Edition, April 2016
1 3 5 7 9 10 8 6 4 2
FAC-020093-16057

Library of Congress Catalog Card Number: 2015936651
ISBN 978-1-4847-2959-5

disneybooks.com
disney.com/alice

Book design by Megan Youngquist Parent

THIS LABEL APPLIES TO TEXT STOCK

Prologue

1868, Strait of Malacca

BOOM! BOOM! Cannon fire exploded in the dark, stormy sky.

With a howl, the wind pushed the *Wonder*, as though helping it dodge the missiles. Rushing along its damaged deck, sailors secured loose lines and fought to keep the clipper afloat.

The moon broke through the clouds, illuminating the three large Malayan junks bearing down on the *Wonder*, their cannons blazing. Above the decks, their red sails cut the sky like shark fins and their masts flew black flags broken only by a wicked devil's face. These pirates would show no mercy.

After cresting an enormous wave, the clipper slipped into a trough, briefly sparing its sailors the sight of their pursuers. But the view ahead was no better.

The jagged outline of an island reared up in front of the *Wonder*. Rings of broken rock shoals—perfect for grounding ships—surrounded it.

His arms straining, the helmsman wrestled with the steering wheel as cannonballs whistled through the air. Debris rained down on him, shattering the chronometer.

"Sir!" the helmsman shouted to the first mate. "We've lost the clock! We cannot reckon our position through the shoals!"

The first mate braced himself as a geyser of water splashed the deck. Scanning the deadly outcroppings ahead of the clipper, he felt a rush of despair. It was no use: the *Wonder* was being herded into a trap. He turned to a figure behind him.

Prologue

"Captain, we must surrender!" the first mate cried. "Or we shall all be lost!"

Alice Kingsleigh stepped out of the shadows, her face fierce and determined. She had not worked so hard or traveled so far to lose everything. And she would not give in to flea-infested pirates.

"I'm not sure surrendering my father's ship guarantees survival, Mr. Phelps," she said calmly.

Alice glanced down at the sextant in her hand, measuring the angle of the moon, and then eyed the barrier shoals ahead. A thrill ran through her as she spotted something her first mate had missed.

"Dead ahead! Full sail!" she cried.

Her crew stared at her in disbelief. Had their captain gone mad?

Mr. Phelps tried to reason with her. "Captain! The shoals . . . the ship will founder! That's impossible!"

"You know my views on that word, Mr. Phelps!"

Alice shot him a stern look. Her father had taught her long ago that anything was possible, and Alice's own adventures had proven that time and again.

The first mate's shoulders sagged, but he nodded and turned to yell at the crew. They scrambled to unfurl the sails fully, and the clipper sped toward the shallows surrounding the island.

"Hard to starboard, Harper!" Alice shouted at the helmsman.

"To starboard? We'll surely capsize!" Harper cried.

"Exactly, Harper. Exactly . . ." Alice said. Her eyes were lit with certainty. Harper had never known his captain to be wrong, so he pulled the ship to the right, gritting his teeth.

The *Wonder* began to tip to the side even as it barreled toward the rocks. *This has to work,* Alice thought. Her mad plan was their only hope. But as Alice calculated their trajectory, she realized it wouldn't be enough. Looking skyward, she spotted a young sailor struggling to unfurl the topsail.

"Secure yourselves, men," Alice called as she raced to a halyard. "We're going to roll!" Grabbing hold of the rope, she slashed it with her sword. Alice's eyes shone as the rope lifted her off the deck and carried her to the top of the *Wonder*. She danced through the rigging and severed the lines keeping the topsail closed. With a whoosh, the sail unfurled and snapped full in the raging wind.

Here we go! Alice thought as the *Wonder* leaned fully horizontal and the mast she clung to dipped into the frigid ocean waves. The keel of the ship scraped along a sandy shoal; then a wave lifted it and pushed it beyond the barrier into calmer waters.

Alice scrambled to reach the mainsails and used her sword to cut them. The sails slumped like weary travelers. Without the full force of the storm behind it, the *Wonder* swung upward, righting itself.

Pushing her wet hair out of her face, Alice looked back. A fearsome grin spread across her features. The larger Malayan ships had splintered into pieces on the shoals. She'd done it. She'd saved her ship, her cargo, and her crew. Relief bled through her, untying the knot she'd been carrying in her stomach.

A cheer rose from her crew as she slid down to the deck. Were it not for her, they would be dead, and they knew it. Stepping forward, Mr. Phelps bowed his head in admiration.

"The only way to achieve the impossible is to believe it *is* possible," Alice told him, thinking of her father's ever-optimistic spirit.

She fished her beloved pocket watch from her cloak and gazed at its inscription: *Charles Kingsleigh, Esq.* If only he could be by her side. Still, she could imagine him looking down at her with pride.

A splatter of rain on her cheek brought Alice

back to the present. She stepped across the deck and hung her pocket watch in front of the broken chronometer.

"I trust this will guide us home," she said. As her crew turned the *Wonder* toward London, Alice added softly under her breath, "It always has. . . ."

I

Four Months Later
London

THE *WONDER* SAILED up the Thames into the heart of London. Lining the shores like sentinels, factories and warehouses crowded together along the river, the streets between them twisting away around tight corners.

Collecting her things, Alice moved about the captain's cabin. She tucked her father's watch into her coat pocket, even though it had stopped working a week earlier. Ever since her father had passed away, Alice had carried the pocket watch with her everywhere, almost like a talisman. While its hands were sadly frozen still, it made her feel closer to him.

She scanned her cabin one last time, then headed up to watch the *Wonder* pull alongside a pier. Satisfied that her crew was properly directing the dockworkers unloading the *Wonder*'s precious cargo, she turned her attention to the wharf.

A slender figure in a gray cloak caught her eye. With a cry of joy, Alice darted down the gangplank.

"Mother!" Alice called as she ran toward her.

Flinging her arms around her mother, she pulled her into a tight embrace. Helen Kingsleigh returned the hug a bit more stiffly, softly patting Alice on the back. She would never get used to her younger daughter's enthusiastic displays of affection, but she was glad to have her back. Every day she'd been gone had been filled with a lifetime of worry.

"Well, here you are . . . finally," Helen said as she stepped away.

Alice drew a breath to launch into stories of her

exploits—she had so much to tell her mother—but she stopped short as an unfamiliar man approached them.

He was young and handsome. His wavy blond hair was neatly combed to the side, and his eyes were a startling blue. As Alice studied his simple, clean suit for a clue, she noticed the insignia stamped on a briefcase he carried. So he was from the firm, here to check up on her cargo.

"You and the *Wonder* have been expected a year, Miss Kingsleigh," he said.

Alicc blushed guiltily, although she felt a twinge of annoyance that he hadn't addressed her as "Captain." It was tiresome to return to England, where her position suddenly eroded to that of a young, unmarried woman. In every port abroad she'd been greeted with far more respect.

Straightening her shoulders, she faced the stranger. "There were . . . complications," she said. She doubted anyone else could have achieved what she had, and Lord Ascot would be pleased with her discoveries, despite the delay.

"I daresay the cargo will account for time," the man responded quickly, noting Alice's stiffness. "I'm James Harcourt, ma'am. Clerk to the firm." He held out his hand and Alice shook it, softening a bit as James nodded respectfully.

"I should like to see Lord Ascot," Alice said as the clerk led her and her mother to a hansom cab.

Pausing at the cab's door, James gazed at her solemnly. "Ah, I'm afraid Lord Ascot passed away whilst you were at sea."

Stunned, Alice turned to her mother, who nodded sadly in confirmation. Alice bowed her head, the loss weighing on her. Lord Ascot had been a singular man. There weren't too many British shipping company presidents who would have taken a chance on her. But he had been more than a generous patron; he'd been a friend to her father and to her.

Chapter One

"The title has passed to his son," James continued.

"Hamish?" Alice struggled to hide her astonishment.

"Indeed, now also chairman of the board," James said.

Alice would not have been more shocked if the clerk had climbed atop the hansom and belted out "God Save the Queen." She could not picture Hamish—droopy-faced Hamish—in charge of anything, much less the company her father had begun. She clambered into the hansom, mulling over the news.

Of course the title and company shares would have passed to Hamish, but he'd always been so uninterested in business matters that his father had given up trying to involve him. Hamish was more concerned with mastering the latest dance step or finding the perfect wife to parade around. Thank God Alice had turned him down; they would have been a terrible pair! She hoped they'd be able to work together. Perhaps the years had changed him. Perhaps he had grown up. At the very least, she hoped he would stay out of her way as she broadened the company's trade routes.

Deep in thought, she was oblivious to the blue butterfly struggling to keep up with the cab.

When they pulled up to her childhood home, Alice sat forward. The redbrick townhouse was just as she'd remembered, even after three years away. She followed her mother inside.

With a decisive click, the front door swung shut just before the blue butterfly reached it. The creature seemed almost to swat angrily at the solid wood before fluttering up to a window instead. Its wings beat soundlessly against the glass.

Alice stood in the front hall, a bit disappointed. While the outside remained the same, the interior was dark and cold. No fires had been lit to welcome them home and the air felt dusty.

"Where's Mary?" Alice asked.

"I'm afraid I let Mary go. I'm perfectly capable of keeping house myself," Helen said.

She reached for Alice's bag, as Mary would have done, to take it up to her room, but Alice picked it up first. She couldn't let her mother serve her.

Shivering slightly, Alice stepped toward the drawing room, planning to light a fire herself, but the sight of the room stopped her short. Half the furniture was missing, including the large red couch and the overstuffed velvet chair she'd always loved. Even the sideboard table was gone, an imprint of its outline on the floor the only sign it had ever been there at all.

Her mother smiled awkwardly at Alice's confused expression and headed downstairs.

"Always warmer down here," she offered.

Once inside the basement kitchen, Helen plucked cups and saucers from the cupboards and set them out for tea. Alice spotted new lines on her mother's face and streaks of gray in her hair. Frowning, she peered at her more closely. Helen's slender frame was thinner than before, and her hands shook slightly as she lifted the steaming kettle off the stove. Time seemed to be taking its toll on her.

"Now then," Helen said, breaking the silence. "Your letters were so infrequent. I hardly know where you have been all this time."

"Oh, Mother! The *Wonder* brought back a hundred kinds of tea from China!" Alice began eagerly, setting aside her worries about her mother for the moment. "And silks of colors you've never seen before. I met with emperors and beggars . . . holy men . . . and pirates!"

Helen's smile disappeared.

"Were you never afraid?" Helen asked worriedly. She poured the hot water into a teapot.

"When I was, I thought of Father," Alice said. She settled into a wooden rocking chair near the stove.

"You sound like him. He'd be so proud. But, my dear, an extra year? At my age you realize that time is a cruel master."

Alice absently rubbed her fingers over her father's pocket watch. "And a thief to boot," she murmured darkly. Time was no friend of hers, having stolen her father too young. "The best are taken first."

Helen turned back to the tea. "And the dregs left behind, I suppose?" she muttered to herself. She shook her head and lifted the tea tray, determined to be cheerful.

"I hear the Ascots are marking Hamish's succession tonight," Helen said as she sank into an armchair opposite her daughter.

"Perfect. We should go," Alice said. She needed to establish her working relationship with Hamish, and there was no time like the present.

"Without an invitation?" Helen blinked at her daughter, her brow furrowed.

"Lady Ascot once said we would always be welcome." Alice waved her hand nonchalantly.

"But, Alice . . ." her mother began.

"Besides, I have a proposition for Hamish," Alice continued.

Helen pursed her lips. "He married last year, Alice. He seems to have gotten over your public rejection—although I would imagine the other three hundred guests might still remember it."

"A *business* proposition, Mother!" Alice nearly rolled her eyes. Then she sat forward, unable to contain her excitement. "It's time we saw the world as our partner, not a pocket to be picked. When I return to China, I'll prove it's so."

"You aim to leave so soon?" As though she could fend off her daughter's departure as well as the cold, Helen drew her shawl tightly. She gathered her next words carefully. "There are matters here that would benefit from your attention."

Alice patted her mother's hand reassuringly. "After my next voyage, you won't have to worry anymore. About anything."

"Am I permitted to worry tonight?" Helen asked.

Answering her mother with only a grin, Alice set off upstairs.

Helen sighed. She had recognized the twinkle in her daughter's eye. If she knew Alice, whatever happened that evening would be memorable, to say the least.

Alice carried her luggage up to her childhood room and pushed open the door. It was like stepping directly into the past.

Her favorite doll was propped up on the bed, and her collection of seashells cluttered a side table. The air still held the scent of lily of the valley from a perfume bottle Alice had "borrowed" from her sister and accidentally broken.

Plunking down her bag, Alice wandered to the writing desk. She picked up a sampler she'd made at age twelve. The embroidery on the alphabet at the top was a little shaky, but she'd taken more time with the center, where the stitches perfectly formed her father's favorite motto: "Six Impossible Things Before Breakfast." Sighing softly, she brushed her fingers over the blue thread, then set the sampler aside.

She found a stack of drawings and watercolors of Underland. She smiled as she thumbed through them. Each of them came to life in her hands as the vivid memories replayed in her mind.

There was the garden of talking flowers and the odd assortment of creatures she'd met there: a dodo bird; Mallymkun, the Dormouse; the Tweedle brothers—Tweedledum and Tweedledee—and, of course, McTwisp, the White Rabbit, who had led her to Underland twice.

In another painting, the Tweedles escorted her through a field of giant mushrooms. They'd been on their way to talk to Absolem, the wise Caterpillar, to determine whether Alice was, in fact, *the* Alice. It had been a hotly debated subject. With a jaunty wink and a broad grin, Chessur, the Cheshire Cat, stared up at her from another page. But the next one she turned to made her shudder.

The deadly dragon, the Jabberwocky, crouched atop some crumbling ruins. It spread its black wings wide, and its tail whipped through the sky. Alice had volunteered to be the White Queen's champion to face the loathsome beast. It remained the scariest thing she'd ever done. Only her faith in the impossible's being possible had carried her through it. Well, that and the enchanted Vorpal sword, which had ultimately helped her slay the Jabberwocky.

Alice flipped to a more peaceful painting. She

and the Mad Hatter stood on the polished white stone balcony at Marmoreal Castle, a series of waterfalls sparkling in the distance.

Hatter turned to the Alice in the painting. "You would have to be half mad to dream me up," he said.

"I must be, then," the watercolor Alice responded.

Hatter and Alice smiled at each other.

Alice recited the next words along with her painted self: "I'll miss you when I wake up."

It was true: she had missed Hatter dearly the past three years. His odd view of the world had blended well with her fierce streak of individuality. And he would have loved to visit all the exotic places she had seen. Every time she had encountered a new fashion style (particularly a hat) or tasted a unique tea, she had thought of him. If only he could have joined her.

Her father, the only person who would have believed her stories of Underland, was gone. And despite everything she had accomplished in *this* world, including her voyages at sea and her captain's title, her mother still only saw her as someone in need of a husband. Her sister, on a mission to spread Christianity in Africa, agreed, no doubt.

Pulling back the curtain from a window, Alice stared out over the rooftops of London. Why was it so hard for her family to accept her? Couldn't they see she was meant for grand adventures? Well, if they needed more proof, Alice would give it to them . . . starting with her meeting with Hamish. Once she had the company's support for her new trade partnerships and she could establish herself and her mother in style, her family would have to acknowledge she'd chosen wisely. It would just take a little more time.

II

THE ASCOT mansion perched atop a hill at the end of a long driveway. Dozens of lanterns shone in the twilight, turning the estate into a twinkling beacon. But as the hansom cab carried the Kingsleighs up the drive, Alice's eyes were drawn instead to the rambling woods lining the road. Leaning forward in excitement, she recognized the gnarled tree that marked the entrance to Underland.

"Look, Mother! The rabbit hole!" Alice said.

"Please don't start that, dear." Helen Kingsleigh's

hand floated up to her forehead, as though she had a headache.

Alice sat back quietly. She knew it was hard for her mother to believe in impossible things. There was no point in pushing the issue.

The carriage pulled to a stop, and a footman rushed forward to open the door and help the ladies out. While Alice paid the driver, the footman took her mother's coat. Picking at the worn lace of her blue dress, Helen wished she'd had something nicer in her wardrobe. Her grimace deepened when she saw the footman's reaction to Alice's outfit.

"I do wish you'd worn that yellow dress," Helen muttered to her daughter as they approached the mansion.

Alice grinned, running her hands down the traditional Chinese silk costume she'd chosen for the occasion. The collar was cut to imitate the petals of a flower, in panels of pink, yellow, and red, and beautifully embroidered butterflies circled the purple jacket. Hanging straight down from her waist, a pleated skirt of green and yellow fabric swung cheerfully against her legs. She knew nobody in London would combine those colors, let alone wear that style, but she adored it.

"If it's good enough for the Dowager Empress of China, it's good enough for the Ascots," Alice said.

"Alice, must you be so headstrong?" Shaking her head, Helen sighed as they swept inside the mansion, servants slamming the grand oak doors behind them. Unbeknownst to the servants, they'd closed the doors in the face of the blue butterfly, who fluttered crossly.

Inside, Alice strode toward the grand hall, her mother lagging self-consciously behind her. They paused in the entryway.

Dressed in their finest, London's elite flittered about on the gleaming floor. A parade of colors from gold to dark blue bustled past as the ladies sauntered by, their hair pinned up and the skirts of their dresses trailing behind them. The men wore tuxedos and white gloves; their backs couldn't have been straighter if each had had a board tied to his spine.

Alice's lips twitched as a flock of peacocks and toddling penguins came to mind.

"Miss Kingsleigh?" someone called. Turning, Alice saw James Harcourt, the clerk, approaching. "What are you—"

"I've come to give my report to Lord Ascot, Mr. Harcourt," Alice said.

James swallowed his words, impressed once again by Alice's cool composure. He nodded and gestured for them to follow him.

They wove through the crowd, and a ripple of whispers followed in their wake as guests raised their eyebrows and muttered about Alice's costume.

Helen wrung her hands in embarrassment, but Alice couldn't have cared less.

Under a shimmering chandelier, they found Lady Ascot, Hamish, and his wife, all smiling benevolently at their audience. Hamish's chest was puffed out in self-importance. At his side, his prim and proper wife, Alexandra, balanced their son in her arms.

That night they were celebrating Hamish's success. Now that he was a lord, nobody could laugh at him ever again. Nobody would dare spurn him the way Alice Kingsleigh once had.

His piggish eyes landed on Helen Kingsleigh and the oddly dressed woman with her. That tiresome clerk, Harcourt, was leading them toward him. Blinking in shock, Hamish realized that the figure in the garish tunic was none other than Alice herself.

Lady Ascot noticed the two interlopers as well.

She could not imagine why they had come uninvited, but she knew it must be Alice's influence. Still, she was too much of a lady to turn them away

"Helen! What a surprise!" Lady Ascot pronounced, her eyebrows raised ever so slightly to register her disapproval of their breach in etiquette. She reached forward with her scarlet-gloved hand—dyed to match her dress perfectly—and clasped Helen's arm before turning to her daughter. "And is that *Alice*? My, the sea and salt air have done wonders for you. When you left, you were so pale and peaked."

"Thank you," Alice said. Only Lady Ascot could find a way to combine an insult with a compliment.

"And, Helen, dear." Lady Ascot turned and noted the weathered velvet of the other woman's gown. "You look . . . well." She smiled politely.

Finally having collected himself, Hamish cleared his throat. "Alice! Welcome home. Only a year late." He rocked on his feet. "We were afraid you may never come back with our ship!"

"*My* ship," Alice said, correcting him. "Hello, Hamish."

Next to them, Alexandra sniffed loudly. "It is proper to refer to my husband as Lord Ascot. It is why we are having this little soiree, after all," she said, her words clipped.

The baby chose that moment to squirm in her arms. Alexandra quickly held him out to the waiting nanny, who swept him off before he could dirty his mother's gown.

"Miss Kingsleigh," Hamish said formally. "This is my wife, the new Lady Ascot."

Alice and Alexandra eyed each other. Alexandra's lips seemed to be permanently pinched together as though she had tasted something bitter.

"So. Hamish tells me you've traveled the world these last three years," Alexandra drawled.

"Yes, I have just returned," Alice replied.

"Well, then! How was it?" Alexandra said.

"The world?" Alice asked.

"Yes!" Alexandra said brightly.

Alice paused to consider. Alexandra struck her as someone satisfied with an altogether ordinary life, yet Alice couldn't help teasing her. "Highly enjoyable. You should visit it sometime."

Behind her, James covered his mouth to muffle his laugh as Alexandra's face registered her astonishment.

"I've come to give my report, Lord Ascot," Alice continued smoothly.

"Ah, of course," Hamish said. "If you would follow me, Miss Kingsleigh." After nodding to his mother and wife, he guided Alice down a hall.

As she followed him, Alice could feel the waves of disapproval from Alexandra, as though it were terribly undignified for a woman to meddle in business affairs. *Yes, she's just the sort of proper society lady Hamish should have as a wife,* Alice thought. *Far better her than I.*

Hamish led Alice to the mansion's smoking room, which was covered in red wallpaper. Portraits of Hamish's ancestors frowned down from their spots on the walls, as if they could smell the smoke puffed up from the pipes of the men gathered below.

The entire room of white-haired gentlemen turned to regard the newcomers. They greeted Hamish with a nod, but they stared blankly at Alice.

"Gentlemen," Hamish said, addressing the room. "Might I introduce Miss Alice Kingsleigh. Miss Kingsleigh—the board."

Despite Alice's polite smile, none of the men's expressions changed. Of course, she hadn't expected it would be easy to win them over. Undaunted, she plunged forward with her planned speech.

"Gentlemen, we must move quickly! The profits of my voyage—"

"Scarcely outweigh the costs," Hamish interjected.

Alice glanced at him. "Further expeditions to Ta-Kiang or Wuchang—" she began.

"There will be no 'further expeditions,'" Hamish interrupted once more.

"What?" Alice was flabbergasted. What could he mean? Surely the company was not going to abandon the trade liaisons she had fostered.

"The risks are not worth the reward," Hamish proclaimed. He shot the board members a quick glance to see if they were admiring his commanding presence.

Her brows creased in confusion, Alice shook her head. The cargo she had brought back was of the finest quality, and there were still many ports to explore. If he would just give her a chance to explain . . . "But you have only to go and see. There are risks, indeed, but the possibilities are limitless."

Hamish waved her words off. "An extra year at sea, Alice. There were hard decisions in your absence. From everyone." As though he were posing for a painting, he clasped his hands behind his back and lifted his head slightly.

Alice stared at him, finally realizing just how deadly serious he was. Nothing she could say would sway him; he had made up his mind. "But . . . what am I to do?"

"There's a position in our clerking office," Hamish offered. His mouth twitched smugly, and Alice realized how much he was enjoying the situation. "You'll start in files, but, in time—"

Alice felt her face burning, anger rising inside her. "This isn't about China at all, is it? It's because three years ago I turned you down when you asked me to marry you!" She couldn't believe Hamish would be so stupid, so pigheaded!

"I'm sorry, Miss Kingsleigh," Hamish said, sounding completely unremorseful. A flush crept up his neck at the mention of her refusal. "But that is all we can do for you. No other company is in the business of hiring female clerks, let alone ship's captains!"

Several of the board members chuckled, while others harrumphed at the thought. Only James, who had slipped into the room behind Alice, stood by quietly, wishing there were something he could do.

Alice ignored the laughter and pounded her hand on a nearby cigar table. Whatever it took, she would make herself heard. "I have voting rights and ten percent of the company! Your father set those shares aside for me—"

"Correction," Hamish proclaimed. "He gave them to your mother, who sold them to me last year, while you were gone. Along with the bond on the house."

Alice's anger seeped out like air from a deflating balloon. "Her . . . house?"

"Secured by your father against the ship he bought," Hamish confirmed.

"The *Wonder*?" Alice's words came out strangled.

"Yes. Sign it over and you'll redeem the house, receive a salary and a pension." His tone might have been bored, but his eyes were fixed intently on her.

"Give up the *Wonder*?" Alice was aghast.

"Otherwise we cannot help you," Hamish said, tapping a slip of paper that had been laid out on a table.

With a new rush of rage, Alice realized it must be a prepared contract for the *Wonder*. Helen Kingsleigh cautiously entered the room at that moment and glanced around.

"Or your mother." Hamish's words sent a chill

through Alice. She spotted Helen's thin shoulders from the corner of her eye, but she spun away, needing time to think.

Shoving open the door, Alice stalked out of the room. Helen raced after her, but Alice didn't stop until Helen reached out and grabbed hold of her sleeve.

Alice turned on her, unable to contain her aggravation. Now they had no say in the company, no control in their fate. "How could you sell our shares?"

"I had no choice, Alice! With your sister on her mission and you at sea for an extra year . . . What was I to do?" Helen's voice climbed higher and people started to turn toward them.

Taking a deep breath, Helen pulled Alice into a hallway, firmly shutting the door behind them for privacy. Artwork lined the walls, interrupted only by a row of windows. Alice tugged away from her mother and stared through the glass at the garden below, where moonlight cast long shadows.

"I did it for you, Alice!" her mother said fervently. "So you can make a decent start in life. So that you won't be alone."

Alice faced her mother. "Ten minutes ago I was a sea captain." Her voice was tinged with bitterness. Her next voyage abroad could have secured them both a comfortable living.

"A sea captain is no job for a lady!" Helen countered.

"Good!" Alice exclaimed. "All the better! On the ocean I am free, as father was. Or would you rather have me be a clerk?"

"I'm talking about marriage, Alice," Helen said impatiently. "Time is against you, and you are being careless with it!"

Not this again, Alice thought. Her mother did not understand that Alice's thirst for adventure meant she could never be content to sit quietly, tending a home for a husband, as was expected. Moments like these were when Alice felt her father's absence all the more keenly. He would have understood how she felt. He would have cheered her on as she took a different path.

"I once believed I could do six impossible things before breakfast," Alice said softly, remembering how her father's face used to light up as he regaled her with fanciful stories of his trips to the moon. Without realizing it, Alice rubbed the spot on her arm where the Bandersnatch's claws had left scars, a permanent reminder of a place where anything might happen.

"That is a child's dream, Alice," her mother said. "The only way for women like us to have a good life is to marry well."

Alice rolled her eyes, her anger returning. Why was her mother so closed-minded? The world was changing. You didn't have to believe in magic to envision new possibilities.

"I'm only trying to help you," her mother said softly.

"Well, don't," Alice snapped. "Because the last thing I want in life is to end up like you."

Alice spun on her heel and stalked off, her words hanging in the air behind her. She didn't turn back, so she didn't see her mother lift her hand to her mouth, tears filling her eyes.

III

A RUSTLING OF LEAVES AND the sweet scent of flowers welcomed Alice as she entered the Ascot greenhouse. Pushing past tropical palm fronds, she wandered to a white metal bench. Through the glass roof, the moon and stars shone down on her. *Almost like being back at sea,* Alice thought as she gazed skyward.

Of course, Alice might never sail again. She sighed as she sat down, then pulled out her father's pocket watch.

"Sign over the *Wonder* to become a clerk . . . and just give up on the impossible?" she said to

herself. She shook her head fiercely. The thought was unbearable. If only Lord Ascot were still alive! With Hamish in charge, Alice might have to give up on her dream and her father's legacy.

A flicker of movement caught her eye as a blue butterfly landed on a nearby orchid. As she turned to gaze at it, it lifted off and flew closer, brushing past her nose and circling her head before landing on the arm of the bench, a hairsbreadth away from her hand. Shimmering in the moonlight, the butterfly's wings flapped open and closed several times, as if it was trying to send her a message.

What a curious creature, Alice thought. She'd never seen a butterfly behave this way. Its gorgeous, bright blue hue reminded her of Absolem's coloring. In fact, the last time she'd spoken to him, back in Underland, he'd been building a chrysalis, so it was *possible* this was him. It definitely wasn't *impossible*, anyway.

"Absolem?" she asked tentatively.

With a flutter, the insect launched into the air and

hovered in front of her face, as if in confirmation, before swooping toward the greenhouse exit. Alice got to her feet and followed it. If it *was* Absolem, perhaps he was trying to lead her back to Underland. But instead of heading for the woods and the rabbit hole, the butterfly flew steadily toward the mansion.

Alice felt a burst of disappointment. She would so have enjoyed a trip to Underland, where nobody would think twice about a female captain. Her friends there would roar in sympathy to hear someone was trying to take her ship away.

The butterfly paused in midair and turned to her. It wove through the air, first toward her and then back toward the house, rather insistently. *Hmm. An irritable butterfly. Yes, that seems like Absolem. Well, even if he's not leading me to Underland, I've nothing better to do,* Alice thought with a shrug.

Wading across the grass, Alice let the butterfly lead her up to the mansion's wide stone steps and back through the open patio doors. Now she was almost positive it was Absolem and that he needed her to follow him. Why else would a butterfly brave the noise and lights of a party? Swooping upward, the butterfly was able to float above the musicians and couples on the dance floor. Alice, however, had to dodge around the dancers to keep it in sight. A gentleman harrumphed as she bumped into him, and she paused to apologize.

By the time she turned back, the butterfly was gone. *Absolem, I can't follow you if you don't slow down!* Scanning the room carefully, she noticed a bright spot of blue on the chandelier above the dining room table. Alice hurried over and, heedless of propriety, climbed up onto first a chair and then the table itself. What could Absolem want? It must be important for him to have left Underland. She stepped over the silverware, which was fanned out on the runner, and edged past arranged plates of fruit, cupcakes, and petit fours and the rose centerpieces lining the table.

Chapter Three

She had almost reached the crystal chandelier when her mother rushed over.

"Alice! Get down from there," Helen ordered in a hushed voice. But it was too late. Already the other guests were falling silent, dumbfounded at the sight of Alice trooping through the desserts.

Perhaps startled by Helen's movement, the butterfly fluttered farther down the table toward the only person who hadn't noticed Alice.

Hamish was busy holding court with the board at the far end of the table. While he didn't see Alice, the butterfly's bright blue wings caught his eye.

"Bloody moths," Hamish complained. He slammed his hand down on the table to smash the insect flat.

"Absolem! No!" Alice shouted. Without thinking, she launched herself off the table onto Hamish, and they both tumbled to the ground.

"Help! Assault! Police! Mother!" Hamish shrieked as Alice's fists pummeled him.

"You brute!" Alice screamed.

"Helen! Control your daughter!" Lady Ascot's tone was aghast.

"Alice! What are you doing?" Helen said, running to them. Her hands reached down toward the tussling pair, but then she pulled back as Alice twisted abruptly.

"Get her off me!" Hamish yelped. He shielded his face as best he could.

Succeeding where Helen had not, a pair of footmen managed to pull Alice off Hamish. Alice saw a flutter of blue near the grand staircase.

Keeping her gaze fixed on the footmen and the stairway beyond, Alice ran her hands over the table behind her. With a surge of hope, she felt a salt and pepper shaker set. She grabbed a shaker in each hand and flung them forward, coating the footmen in the spices. The men doubled over, sneezing fiercely. Alice ducked past them and bounded up the stairs, calling for Absolem to wait for her.

Chapter Three

Alice rounded the corner at the top of the stairs, but the butterfly had disappeared. She dashed down the hallway, but at the sound of men thumping up the stairs behind her, she ducked into the nearest room and locked the door.

Alice waited as the men pounded down the hall, their footfalls making the floor vibrate. As they passed, she let out her breath. Only then did she turn to survey the room.

It was a parlor, but clearly one that hadn't been used in a long while. A cluttered desk sat to the side; a chess set on a table was covered in dust; and the woven rugs let off a moldering smell.

Dominating one wall were two oil portraits and a giant antique mirror, which hung above a fireplace. The immense white marble mantelpiece was inlaid with green stone. On top, the exposed silver cogs of a clock ticked under a bell-shaped glass.

A movement in the mirror caught her eye. The blue butterfly flitted toward her.

"*Absolem?* It *is* you, isn't it?" Alice exclaimed as the insect landed on her shoulder. His antennae waved at her before he lifted off again.

As Alice twisted to watch the butterfly, she noticed that something was happening to the mirror above the fireplace. Before her eyes, the glass began to fog up and evaporate into a glowing silvery mist.

Absolem flew toward it, and instead of slamming against the surface, he made his way straight into the swirling looking glass.

Alice gasped as the butterfly's silhouette appeared in the reflection of the room. She spun around; there was no butterfly in the parlor with her. Puzzled, she turned back to the looking glass. Absolem had glided to a rest on the chess table in the reflection.

"Curious," she whispered to herself. Nearing the fireplace, she reached toward the mirror.

The glass felt like a cool pond of water, her

fingers passing through it with no resistance. When she pulled her hand back, she was surprised to find it was dry.

Someone rattled the doorknob of the parlor and Alice whirled. Through the thick oak of the door, she could hear men in the hallway calling for the key.

Not wanting to face them, Alice quickly climbed up onto the mantelpiece, careful not to jar the surely priceless vase balanced on the edge. She hesitated before the mirror, the clock next to her ticking much more loudly all of a sudden. Taking a deep breath, she stepped through the looking glass just as a key jingled in the lock behind her.

A ripple of coolness broke over Alice's skin as she passed through the mirror, but no droplets of water or mist clung to her. She emerged on the other side, where the room was much larger than she'd anticipated—a giant replica of the parlor she had just left—and where she was the size of a large insect. She was standing on the marble mantelpiece, her head reaching only halfway up the clock. The walls and ceiling—not to mention the floor—seemed impossibly far away.

"Curiouser and curiouser," she said, a bolt of déjà vu flowing through her as the words left her mouth. Only Underland made her feel this excited and disoriented at the same time.

"Hello again, Alice!" chimed a voice.

Alice turned to discover the clock on that side of the mirror featured an old man's face. As he smiled at her, the numbers next to his mouth lifted higher.

"You shouldn't be here," the lady in the oil painting whined. "You're too old for this nonsense!"

"Oh, hush," countered the man in the painting opposite her. "One is never too old!"

Ignoring the woman, Alice smiled gratefully at the two gentlemen. She gathered a deep breath and stepped off the mantelpiece, then plummeted to the cushioned bench surrounding the fireplace.

Her feet sank into the soft cloth as she made her way toward the distant chess table.

Alice noticed a round egg man with cracks all over his face resting on the table's edge. It could only be one fellow: Humpty Dumpty. He gave her an encouraging wave. With a running start, she leapt for the table, her arms pinwheeling as she landed.

Unfortunately, one of her arms brushed against the egg man and he began to teeter. Alice regained her balance just as Humpty Dumpty wobbled forward.

"Not again! Uh . . . uh . . . ooohh!" he cried as he tumbled to the floor. Alice winced as he shattered into pieces.

"Sorry!" she cried guiltily. "I'm so sorry!"

"Don't worry, dear!" Humpty's disembodied face called up to her. "I really ought to stop sitting on walls."

One of the chess kings charged over and peered off the edge next to Alice. Turning, the king bellowed at his team, "All my horses, all my men! To the rescue!" The chess pieces obediently swarmed around Alice and began to slide down the long table legs to the ground. There they began sorting through the bits of Humpty Dumpty's shell, matching them up as best they could.

Alice followed the chess men down the table leg, apologizing as she went. Poor Humpty!

The butterfly landed on the floor beside her. His blue wings shimmered, but his face held its usual disapproving frown. "Clumsy as always, and twice as dim," he drawled. "I thought you'd never get the idea."

"Oh, Absolem," Alice cried happily. "It *is* you!" She flung her arms around him, and the Butterfly's face softened even as he wriggled away.

"You've been gone too long, Alice. Friends cannot be neglected," he said.

"Why? What has happened?" asked Alice in alarm.

Absolem lifted off into the air. "All will become clear in the fullness of time. For now, hurry, follow that passage." His antennae waved toward the far door.

Shaking her head at his vagueness, she started across the room. Clearly Absolem's metamorphosis into a butterfly had not made him more forthright. As she reached the door, Alice felt her luck turn. The door was just her size. As she opened it, she heard Absolem's voice, and she turned to look over her shoulder.

"Do mind your step," Absolem called out as Alice stepped through the doorway . . . and straight into thin air.

IV

"AAAAAAAAHHHHHHHHH!" ALICE screamed as she tumbled through a brilliantly colored sky. Fluffy pink clouds floated serenely by and a few gangly birds squawked as they veered out of her way. Why did she always have to *fall* into Underland? The ground was rushing toward her at an alarming rate, and unlike during her tumble down the rabbit hole, there were no objects to slow her descent.

"*Oof!*" Alice landed with a thud on the petals of a giant chrysanthemum. Sitting up in a daze, she realized the flower stuck out of an arrangement on

a table in the garden of Marmoreal Castle. To her delight, her old friends were gathered around the table, peering down at her.

At the end sat McTwisp, the White Rabbit, who had first led her to that magical place; and Thackery, the wacky March Hare. The Tweedles, bald and roly-poly as ever, rocked slightly on a bench to the side. Opposite them, Bayard, the brown-and-black bloodhound with the sharpest nose in Underland, woofed a low greeting at Alice. Pacing back and forth among the papers scattered on the table was Mallymkun, the fearless Dormouse. And directly in front of Alice, the ever-beautiful and kind face of the White Queen, Mirana, peered down, although her expression looked troubled.

Alice stood and brushed herself off. She beamed up at everyone, but nobody returned her smile.

"Have I come at a bad time?" she asked.

"We were afraid you weren't coming at all," Mirana said somberly. With gentle hands, she moved

Alice down from the centerpiece to rest on the table.

"Whatever's the matter?" Alice said. The Jabberwocky was dead, and with Iracebeth, the Red Queen; and her lackey, Stayne, banished to the Outlands, Alice had hoped Underland would enjoy years of peace.

"The Hatter's the matter," McTwisp said. Alice realized with a jolt that the Mad Hatter was indeed missing—something he would hate. He always loved a good party.

"Or the matter of the Hatter?" Tweedledum said.

"The former!" Tweedledee insisted.

"The latter!" his brother retorted.

"Tweedles!" Mirana's tone was brisk as she shot the boys a warning look.

"He's mad," the Tweedles said in unison.

"Hatter?" Alice said. "Yes, I know. That's what makes him so . . . him." She wished they'd get to the real problem.

"But worse," Tweedledum continued ominously,

bending his head down toward her. "Denies himself laughter."

"Grows darker, less dafter," his brother finished.

The Hatter not laughing? It was hard for Alice to imagine him without a mischievous glint in his eye and a grin on his face. As if summoned by her thoughts, a toothy grin appeared in midair. Slowly, the rest of the Cheshire Cat came into view as he lazily twisted himself into a circle.

"And no scheme of ours can raise any sort of smile," Chessur explained, gesturing to the papers on the table.

Looking down, Alice saw that the pages she stood on were covered with sketches and ideas of ways to make Hatter laugh: diagrams of where to tickle, schemes of how to surprise him, and pages of scribbled jokes and riddles to amuse him.

Chessur's eyes fixed on Alice as he continued: "We'd rather hoped you might help us save him."

Chapter Four

Alice frowned. "Save him? What happened?"

Everyone exchanged looks; then Bayard nosed forward. As he leaned in, Alice got a close-up view of his nostrils, which loomed large next to her shrunken stature.

"There was a great storm and we ventured out on to Tulgey Woods to investigate," Bayard began. He described how the wind had scattered leaves and branches everywhere. As they'd walked along, they had started to play fetch, with Bayard hurling a stick and Hatter bounding after it on all fours, his tongue hanging out sideways.

"Hatter was perfectly Hatterish," Bayard continued, "until . . ."

The hound paused, the skin between his eyes crinkling in concern. He continued, explaining how Hatter had suddenly frozen, all the color draining from his face as though he had seen a ghost. Then Hatter had plucked a tiny hat made out of blue paper from inside a tree stump, where it appeared to have been hidden.

"That was the start of it," Bayard said ruefully.

"Of what?" Alice asked, pressing him.

"The grand decline," Mirana said somberly.

McTwisp hopped forward. "He's convinced his family are still alive."

"Which has made him deadly serious," Bayard went on.

"Terminally sane," Tweedledum intoned. And for once, his brother had nothing to add.

Mallymkun sniffed, then shook her head. As Alice was the same height as the Dormouse, she had no trouble patting Mally on the shoulder. Silence fell over the table, everyone lost in thought.

"We've tried everything," Bayard said finally. He pawed at some of the papers on the table, unearthing a recipe for giggle juice and a scribbled skit entitled *We're Just Mad for Madness!*

Chapter Four

With hopeful eyes, Mirana turned to Alice. "And then we thought of you."

Alice drew herself up tall—well, as tall as she could, given her diminished height. No matter what, she would not let them—and, more importantly, the Hatter—down. "Where is he?" she asked.

After ducking behind a bush, eating a bit of Upelkuchen cake—she knew better than to take large bites—and adjusting her outfit, Alice emerged feeling normal-sized. She nodded at Mirana, who broke into the first smile Alice had seen since she had arrived.

The White Queen then led the way out of the castle's garden and down into a shaded wood. The rest of the gang trailed behind them, with the Tweedles nudging each other out of the way every few steps to get closer to the front.

Mirana stopped at the edge of a clearing

overlooking a canyon. Beautiful cherry blossom trees sprouted along the sheer cliffs facing them, and a small waterfall tinkled merrily down one wall. Straight ahead, a narrow strip of land barely three feet wide stuck out into the canyon and led to a house that could only belong to the Mad Hatter. For one, you'd have to be crazy to risk that path every day. For another, the house was shaped like a top hat, with circular walls and a roof that jutted out like a brim.

With careful steps, Alice picked her way along the path and walked up onto the red-and-white porch. She raised her hand to knock on the bright turquoise door, but it flew open before she could. A man stood there in a neatly pressed dark gray suit. His red hair was combed flat and he wore a serious expression on his face. Blinking, Alice tried to process what her eyes were showing her. It was the Hatter, but it wasn't. He looked completely . . .

normal. If not for the color of his hair, he could have fit in with the bankers in London.

"Yes?" Hatter asked. Even his voice was different—flatter and lower.

"Hatter? It's me . . . Alice!" she said. She stepped forward to hug him, but he shied away, peering behind her anxiously.

"I'm not taking on any new heads now," Hatter said quickly. "Good day."

Ducking backward, he slammed the door in Alice's face. She stared at its wooden planks for a moment, then firmly pushed it open and marched inside. This might prove to be more difficult than she had thought, but he *would* talk to her.

The interior was cozy, with warm wooden floors, and achingly neat. Rolls of fabric filled a set of shelves, all impeccably labeled with their exact colors and materials. Hanging on the walls, examples of the Hatter's past work showed off his skill—the hats all brushed and the feather plumes fluffed to perfection—and a turquoise spiral staircase led up to the next floor.

The Hatter himself had settled in behind a large desk and had his head buried in an accounting ledger, a quill pen in his hand poised over the page. Startled by her entrance, he looked up, eyes wide.

"Hatter, it's me! Alice! *Alice!*" she exclaimed.

"Miss, please." Hatter set down his pen and raised his hands. "If you want a hat—"

"I don't want a hat," Alice said. "I've come to see you. I want to *talk* to you!"

"Well, if you don't want a hat, I'm quite certain I can't help you!" Hatter said matter-of-factly.

"But you *can* help! I'm sure you can." Alice leaned across the desk, searching his face for some spark of recognition. "I just need you to be *you* again! Everyone does."

The Hatter narrowed his eyes at her. "Don't bring any funny ideas here," he said.

Chapter Four

Alice smiled slyly. "Not even if I know how a raven is like a writing desk?"

Hatter's face remained blank.

"Because there is a *b* in both and an *n* in neither," Alice continued.

She grinned triumphantly at him, but Hatter just stood up and turned away. Muttering to himself, he moved through an open doorway to a back room. Disappointed but undeterred, Alice followed him.

In the back parlor, Hatter paused beneath a giant family portrait. The men and women were posed around a tall black top hat that rested on a white stone pillar. Hatter himself stood at one edge of the group. The man closest to him looked stern and was leaning slightly away from Hatter, as though Hatter didn't quite belong with them. All the relatives wore serious expressions except for Hatter and the young baby.

"Was that . . ." Alice began softly.

"My family," Hatter said proudly. "Lost for

many years, but now they're coming home! Look, I've made hats for each of them!"

Turning with a flourish, he gestured to a row of beautifully crafted hats. "My father, Zanik; my mother, Tyva; Uncle Poomally; Aunt Bumalig; Cousins Pimlick, Paloo, and baby Bim." Hatter pointed to each hat in turn, starting with a black top hat bound with a bright red sash and ending with a light blue bonnet.

"But . . . how do you know they're alive?" Alice asked.

Hatter leaned toward her, studying her face.

"Can you keep a secret?" he whispered.

"No," Alice said honestly.

"Good!" Hatter spun around and dug in a drawer. "I found this," he cried, producing a tiny blue paper hat. "Proof! A sign! A message!" He paused, then continued with conviction. "They're alive!"

Alice frowned in dismay: how on earth could a

crumpled paper hat prove his family had survived? "But if they're alive," she said, trying to reason with him, "where are they?"

"That's the trouble, isn't it?" Hatter grumbled, his hands waving in the air. "High and low. I've searched both. Nowhere. Naught. Nothing. I don't understand why they haven't come and found me." His shoulders slumped as he sank onto a chair.

"I don't understand." Reaching forward, Alice touched his back gently. "You yourself told me your family died. Long ago—" She broke off as Hatter stood abruptly.

"I don't know who you are or what you're trying to do"—Hatter's voice rose in agitation—"but my family is not gallsackering dead!"

"Hatter, please," Alice said.

"Get out!" Hatter bellowed. The force of his words caught him off guard and he stumbled back. Alice started forward to help support him, but he shook his head and waved her away. Breathing heavily, he turned and leaned against a table.

Not sure what she could possibly say to fix things, Alice retreated. After one final glance at the Hatter's trembling frame, she ducked through the front room and out into the sunlight.

V

MALLYMKUN and the March Hare sprang to their feet, their faces hopeful, when she emerged. Behind a fretful McTwisp, the Tweedles clustered together with Bayard, and Mirana's arms floated out from her sides as she leaned forward expectantly. Alice felt the weight of her friends' eyes on her.

"He doesn't even know who I am," she admitted mournfully.

At once, the group's faces all fell. Alice bit her lip and trudged dejectedly away from the door. The Hatter had always been so confident in her, even when she wasn't sure of herself. On her last trip to Underland, he'd insisted she was *the* Alice, the one they'd been waiting for, regardless of what anyone else said. Now he treated her like a stranger.

"What's happened to him?" Alice asked.

"It's as we feared." Mirana's voice trembled. "He's caught a terrible case of the Forgettingfulness."

"The Forgettingfulness?" Alice repeated as they headed into the village.

"It's when things go in one ear . . ." Tweedledum pointed to his ear.

"And out the other two," Tweedledee finished, his hands flying away from his head.

"It all goes back to the Horunvendush Day," Mirana said. She stopped by a fountain and waved her hand over the water. In the spray, images of a fairground with colorful booths and smiling people appeared.

"He has always somehow blamed himself for

his family's death," Mirana continued as Alice recognized Hatter's relatives in the scene.

In it, Zanik and Tyva Hightopp stood talking under an old oak tree. His cousins loudly raced past as his aunt and uncle paused next to a DRINK ME stall.

A trumpet blare announced the arrival of Mirana, who rode a white horse, the White Knight and Hatter following on foot behind her. Spotting his family, Hatter tentatively raised one hand to wave just as a dark shadow loomed overhead.

With a defiant shriek, the Jabberwocky dove out of the sky. The dragon seemed just as fearsome as when Alice had faced it. Its skin was dark as pitch and covered in armor-like scales. Its razor-sharp claws swiped through the air. All around the fairground, people screamed and ran for cover.

The Jabberwocky swung its massive head, the crest around its neck flaring as it roared out a stream of fire, lighting up booths and banners. Crackling sounds and smoke filled the air.

As the White Knight charged forward to face the beast, Mirana's horse reared in fright. Hatter lunged for the reins, jerked the horse around, and quickly led it and Mirana away from the clearing. Flames swallowed up the fairground.

Mirana stared into the gurgling water of the fountain, remembering. Hatter had been so brave that day, whisking her away to safety. If only his family had been as fortunate. When Hatter returned to look for them, he had only found ashes.

In the glittering spray of water, the image of a younger Hatter stood among the blackened wreckage of the Horunvendush celebration. His face was pained, matching the devastation that surrounded him.

The image faded and the White Queen turned to Alice with a grave expression. "And he has lived ever since with the weight of their loss," she said.

Chapter Five

Manifesting just over Mirana's shoulder, Chessur's bright green eyes flicked toward Alice. "So you see, dear Alice, like a tree, our present problem has its roots in the past . . ." he said.

"I see," Alice murmured. "I think."

"Which is why we were hoping you might go back into the past and save the Hatter's family," Mirana said, sweeping her hands together and pulling them to her chest.

"Go back in time? But how?" Alice asked. She'd never considered such a thing before. If it was possible—oh, if it was—there were so many moments she'd like to relive! She could see her father again, maybe save him, too. Although, perhaps it was a magic that worked only in Underland.

"The Chronosphere," Chessur said, interrupting her thoughts, his voice loaded with something Alice couldn't quite pin down. Was it awe? Like all the cats she'd ever known, Chessur never seemed to consider anything impressive or superior to himself. For him to use a tone of such deference was unusual . . . and intriguing.

"I'm sorry," Alice said. "The Chrono-what?"

"The Chronosphere. It's the heart that powers Time. Legend has it, it lets one travel across the Ocean of Time," Mirana explained.

Alice looked around at all her friends. McTwisp was fiddling unconsciously with his pocket watch. The March Hare's nose twitched uncontrollably, and Mallymkun glared up at Alice challengingly, as if she thought Alice would refuse to help. Scraping at the gravel of the road, the Tweedles shifted back and forth on their feet, while Bayard gazed at Alice with his large eyes. Floating lazily above them all, Chessur groomed his tail.

"But why me?" Alice asked, turning back to Mirana.

"None of us can use it because we've already been in the past. And if your past self sees your future self . . ." Mirana's voice trailed off.

"Yes?" Alice said, nudging. "What happens if your past self sees your future self?"

"Well, no one actually knows," Mirana admitted. "But we know it's catastrophic."

"It sounds dangerous. And complicated," Alice said.

Chessur popped into the air next to Alice's shoulder, startling her. "It's not *im*possible, merely *un*possible," he said.

Alice paused for a moment, but there was really nothing to think about. "Hatter is Underland, and Underland is Hatter. If he is in need, I will help him, no matter what."

The Tweedles broke into applause. His ears flopping, the March Hare leapt with joy, and Mallymkun nodded approvingly.

Smiling, Mirana took Alice's hands. "We rather hoped you might say that."

As far as Alice was concerned, there was no time to lose. The quicker she could get started, the quicker they'd get their beloved Hatter back. "And where exactly is this 'Chronosphere'?" she asked.

"In the hands of Time, of course," Chessur purred.

"Well, I suppose all things are," Alice said. "But where is it now?"

"In the hands of Time," Mirana repeated. "It's his."

Alice blinked. "I'm sorry. Time is a 'he'?"

Her friends nodded. Alice tried to imagine Time as a person, wasting away hours and minutes, never needing to worry about running out of himself. Or maybe he was vindictive; after all, Time flew when you were having fun, and dragged when you were miserable. Not to mention his habit of taking good people—like her father. Then again, perhaps he was just careless and flighty. You could never find Time when you needed it—him. Well, regardless, she *was* going to convince him she needed to borrow his Chronosphere.

Chapter Five

"So," Alice said to Mirana, "where does Time spend himself?"

Mirana turned and led Alice and the others into Marmoreal Castle. They walked for some time, winding up and down stone stairways and past abandoned tapestries, until they came to a part of the castle Alice had never seen before. The room they entered had a black-and-white marble floor, the tiles spiraling to the center, where the only object in the room stood, tall and imposing.

It was an enormous black grandfather clock whose ticks and tocks echoed loudly in the space. The sound was oddly ominous.

Drawing closer, Alice saw that the clock was bound in dozens of old ropes. Mirana approached it warily, as if the clock might swallow her whole.

"He lives in a void of infinitude. In a castle of eternity. Through here." Mirana gestured at the clock as she spoke. "One mile past the pendulum."

Alice watched the pendulum swing, its rhythm

hypnotic. Only when Mirana stepped between her and the golden arm did Alice snap out of it.

The White Queen waved her hands in the air. "Opening time!" she said. As her fingers traced intricate patterns in front of her, the ropes around the clock began to twist and unravel. Alice gasped as they lifted outward little by little, revealing themselves to be thousands of white butterflies. They swirled around her before fluttering out the far window. Turning to Mirana, Alice raised one eyebrow in an unspoken question.

"Keeps the riffraff out," Mirana said with a shrug. She dug into a pocket of her white dress and drew out a brass key. Carefully, she fitted it into the front of the clock's glass door.

"Everyone, get ready," she said.

And then she turned the key.

As the door opened, a fierce vacuum sucked at the air in the room, pulling it into the clock. Mallymkun clutched at the March Hare's kerchief to keep from being tugged in as well. Even Alice was drawn a step closer to the clock and had to kick her legs apart to brace herself.

Just as quickly as the wind had begun, it fell off. Tentatively, Alice approached the ornate wooden frame of the clock and peered in past the pendulum.

There was no light, just an infinite stretch of darkness. Alice shivered.

To steady herself, she went over her tasks. "Find Time's castle, borrow the Chronosphere, travel back in time to Horunvendush Day. Save the Hatter's family from being killed, and thereby save the Hatter," she muttered.

"Simple . . . seemingly," Chessur said from behind her.

Alice turned to see everyone bunched together, anxious smiles on their faces. Well, she wasn't going to accomplish anything by waiting and worrying. She faced forward again, ready to begin.

Mirana reached out, her hand stopping Alice.

"Time is extremely powerful and apparently quite full of himself," the White Queen warned. "So mind your manners. He is not someone you want as your enemy."

Alice bit her lip. No, she did not want to be on Time's bad side. After nodding first at Mirana, then at the others, she ducked into the clock. As she stepped inside, she heard Bayard call out, "Fairfarren, Alice!" But she dared not look back.

VI

ALICE TEETERED on the edge of a black void. One more step forward and she would have plunged into an infinite abyss. At the thought, her skin broke out in goose bumps, and she rubbed her arms to try to warm herself.

Far across the void, the black spires of a Gothic castle stretched upward. But there was no way to get there. Alice sighed in frustration. The sound was swallowed up quickly, like it had never happened. Then she heard something—a rhythmic beat, like a drum . . . or a clock.

Tick.

Tick.

Peering down, Alice saw a stone walkway yards beneath her and twenty feet away, but it was ticking its way toward her. The length of it reached all the way across the chasm to the castle, and it seemed to shift closer every second. It looked like it was the second hand to an enormous clock with the castle sitting at its center!

Tick.

Tick.

Alice shifted her stance and bent her knees. Ten feet away, then five, four, three . . .

Tick.

Tick.

As the stone hand ticked into place below her, Alice leapt forward. She swayed for a moment, but her years aboard the *Wonder* had given her superb balance, even on moving objects. Brushing her palms together, she strode confidently along the two-foot-wide path toward the castle.

Chapter Six

DONG! Out of nowhere, a thunderous clang rolled across the void, vibrating the walkway beneath her. It felt like an earthquake, and Alice stumbled, her feet slipping off the stone path. Her fingers scrabbled furiously at the gritty surface as she slid over the edge.

At the last second, just when Alice thought time (or rather *Time*) would be the death of her, her hands found the cool stone. *Whew, that was too close,* she thought.

Shifting her weight, Alice started to pull herself up, but the second hand ticked just as she reached forward. She lost her grip, sliding backward until she was dangling from just one hand.

Don't look down—that was what they told people who were afraid of heights. But Alice had never had that phobia. And she had no choice now *but* to look down. Her eyes swept her surroundings as she looked for an escape.

There!

Far below her, she spotted what must be the minute hand. The second hand was ticking her closer to it, second by second. She just had to hang on a bit longer. . . .

Tick.

Her palm holding the stone edge began to sweat.

Tick.

She dug her fingers in, focusing all her energy on holding on tight. She'd never clung to time as desperately as she did then.

Tick.

Alice unfurled her fingers and let go as the second hand lined up with the minute hand. For a breathless second—she knew it was a second exactly, because the hand above ticked the time—she hung almost weightless in the air. Then she smacked down onto the rocky pebbles of the minute hand, landing hard on her bottom.

After taking another few seconds (*tick, tick,*

tick) to catch her breath, she slowly got to her feet. Moving more carefully, she resumed her journey to the castle. Luckily, the minute hand was more stable and a good deal wider, and no more gongs rang out.

At the end of the walkway, she clambered up a set of steps that looked like melted black stone. Soon the huge gates of the castle stood before her. *How tall* is *Time?* she wondered. She'd never felt so small—and that was saying something, considering she'd once been only three inches tall.

Alice stepped up to the door and leaned her body into it.

CRRREEEEEAAAAAAK. With a groan of protest from the hinges, the door swung open.

Beyond it lay a massive hallway with gigantic carved columns soaring toward an arched ceiling. Staring in wonder, Alice passed through them. There were stairways and walkways all over the place.

Letting out a loud squeal, the columns next to her turned. Their bases were actually cogs! The movement set off a chain reaction, rotating enormous gears that sank halfway into the floor.

All around her, the tools of time wound and turned like parts of a well-oiled machine. At the end of the hallway, another immense door loomed. *Time certainly likes to make a grand impression,* Alice thought as she pushed her way into the next room.

Built on the same grandiose scale as the rest of Time's castle, the throne room was a vast obsidian chamber. The ceiling was so far above her Alice could barely see it. Gothic arches lined the walls, with more looping overhead, breaking up the space. Straight in front of her, a large staircase led up to a raised pedestal with a throne. A shaft of light pierced down from directly above the throne.

The man of the hour—and day, and week, and year—was sprawled on the throne. Dark, bushy muttonchops stood out against his pale skin, and a tall black headpiece rose majestically from the top of his head. Sticking out from both sides of his fur-lined cloak were enormous sculpted shoulder pads, almost like wings, which gave his torso an hourglass shape. One of his gloved hands clutched a black scepter, and his eyes were shut tight.

Alice had not expected to find Time sleeping on the job, but then again, it wasn't like he was ever really *off* the clock. And he had to sleep *some*time, she supposed.

For a brief second, one of his eyes cracked open; then it dropped back shut without registering her. Or so she thought. He didn't even twitch as she climbed the staircase toward him.

Then, out of nowhere, Time seemed to jolt awake. Alice practically heard a *boing* of springs and coils jerking his body upright. She took an involuntary step back as his silver eyes fixed on her. Gathering her confidence, she cleared her throat and swept forward. If she could negotiate with the merchants of Hong Kong and visit with the empress of China, she could work out a deal with Time.

"Good day, sir," she said, choosing her words carefully. "I'm so sorry to bother you, but I was wondering if you might have time to speak with me?"

It was a greeting worthy of the most genteel London society. Even her mother could not have found fault with it.

Time chuckled to himself. "Time?" he said. "I have all the time in the world, young lady." He waved his hand languidly in the air. His leather vest creaked as he leaned forward with sudden intensity. "The question is . . . will I spare any for you?"

"That is the question, sir," Alice replied politely.

"Do you promise to be amusing?" Time asked.

"I don't know." Alice's eyebrows furrowed. "It's rather a serious subject."

"Well, I am a rather serious person. For I am Time. The Infinite." His eyes focused on something above Alice's head, as though he was imagining a crowd of admirers. "The Immort—Wait . . . what time is it?"

Bringing her hand to her mouth, Alice muffled a laugh. It was a rather odd question coming from Time himself. Luckily, Time was busy and didn't notice her reaction.

He flung open his vest and peered downward to where, in place of a heart, a beautiful clock ticked in his chest. Time *tsk*ed to himself.

"Hang it all! How infinitely ironic! I'm going to be late!" he cried.

Without a second glance at Alice, he bounced out of his throne and charged toward a door, his long cloak flowing behind him. She ran after him, not wanting to lose Time.

Moving at a brisk clip down an endless hallway,

Time outpaced her with his long legs, and Alice had to hurry to catch up.

"Keep up," Time barked. "You have precisely sixty seconds in eighty-five seconds' time." He squinted at her and nodded in the direction of her pocket. "Why do you carry that fallen soldier?" he asked.

Puzzled, Alice patted her pocket and drew out her father's broken pocket watch. How had he known it was there? "This? It was my father's," she explained.

Time studied it briefly, then turned away. "A fine-looking instrument. Though I'm afraid its time has expired."

She raised her chin. "My father was a great man. His watch reminds me that nothing is impossible. I wouldn't part with it for anything in the world."

"Everyone parts with everything eventually, my dear," Time drawled.

Before she could respond, he spun and pushed

through an intricately carved set of doors into yet another immense room.

"Behold! The Grand Clock of All Time!" he said proudly, stepping onto a balcony overlooking the chamber.

TICKTOCK, boomed the room, which was itself the clock. Gears and cogs of all sizes covered the floor. In the center of it all, sparks of light surrounded a spinning white orb. Without knowing how she knew, Alice recognized it as the Chronosphere.

As she watched, several small mechanical men clambered among the wheels below. Dressed in similar overalls, with various tools hanging around their waists, they seemed interchangeable—except for one, whose spectacles twinkled as he looked up at them. That specific tinkerer tucked a clipboard under his arm, picked his way through the spare parts lying along a walkway, and hustled up the stairs to reach them.

Coming to a halt in front of Time, the man saluted crisply.

Time smiled at him. "Ah. And how is Time, Wilkins?"

"Would you like the long report or the short report, sir?" the foreman asked, glancing down at his clipboard.

"The short report, of course!" Time exclaimed.

"Time is, sir," Wilkins said.

Time clapped his hands together. "Jolly good. Well done, Wilkins! Keep it up."

If that was all there was to say, Alice didn't see the point of asking the foreman to report in. Her gaze returned to the chamber below, where the Chronosphere crackled with energy.

Time noticed Alice looking but misinterpreted the direction of her gaze. He waved at the other men. "Oh, and these fine chaps with Wilkins here are my Seconds."

Chapter Six

As one, the mechanical men jerked toward Time and started bobbing their heads, calling, "Tick, tick, tick, tick." It was rather like listening to an orchestra of cymbals, all clanging together.

Smiling, Time basked in the sound before turning to Alice. "Every Second counts. Never forget that," he said.

Alice nodded, but Time was already moving toward the door. Lingering behind for a moment, she gazed over the Grand Clock, silently studying the Chronosphere. She had found it. Now Alice just had to persuade Time to let her borrow it for a while.

Weaving through a maze of corridors and stairways, she followed Time to a comfortable sitting room. It was the smallest space she'd seen yet in the castle, and the cheery flames in the fireplace and cushion-covered chairs made it also the most welcoming.

Time plopped down into the tallest armchair.

"Now," he said. "Ask your question. You have one minute exactly."

Alice dove in. "It's about the Hatter, Tarrant Hightopp. You see, the Jabberwocky killed—"

Time's eyes began to glaze over. He opened his vest and wound the second hand of his heart clock forward. As he did so, Alice almost tripped over her words as they poured out of her.

"—hisfamily ontheHorunvendushDay. And I'dlikeyourpermission ifyouplease toborrowthe Chronosphere—"

Alice fell silent as Time tensed and held up a commanding hand.

"How do *you* know about the Chronosphere?" Time asked. His face grave, he leaned in toward her.

"That wasn't a minute!" Alice protested.

"What do you know of the Chronosphere?" Time's voice rose and his eyebrows drew together menacingly.

"I'd like to borrow it," Alice said. She clasped

her fingers together in front of her to keep her hands still . . . and to remind herself to stay polite.

"Borrow it? *Borrow it?!*" He leapt to his feet with a cry of outrage, and his moustache bristled, as though it, too, were offended. "The Chronosphere powers Time oneself! It is not something to be 'borrowed,' like a croquet mallet or a pair of hedge clippers!"

"But—" Alice began.

Time whirled and stalked to the door. He jerked it open and pointed imperiously to the hall.

"You are asking me to violate the logic of the Universe," he hissed. "The answer is no."

"But—" Alice tried again.

"You are not amusing," Time said. "Good day."

It was as useless as arguing with the bullheaded Hamish, yet Alice persisted. "But I need the Chronosphere, sir! I need to save my friend!" Couldn't he see how important this was?

"Wilkins!" Time bellowed. The foreman hurried

up. "Escort this trespasser out, if you'd be so kind."

Alice pressed her lips together to hold back what she wanted to say. Instead, she bowed politely and said, "Yes, sir. Sorry to bother you."

As she passed in front of him, Time addressed her once more. "Young lady." She paused to look at him. "You cannot change the past," he said in a gentler tone. "It always was. It always will be. Although, I daresay, you might learn something from it."

"Thank you for your time, sir," Alice said simply. Ducking her head, she turned to follow Wilkins before Time could see the spark of defiance in her eyes.

VII

WILKINS CLANKED along the hallway in front of Alice, leading her through the maze of passageways. Alice stewed behind him, her mind churning. She was not ready to give up on her mission yet.

A shrill voice sang out from somewhere ahead, breaking into Alice's thoughts. "Oh, tick-tock!"

Grinding to an abrupt halt, Wilkins turned to Alice, his face ashen and his eyes blinking rapidly. "Miss, would you mind seeing yourself out?" he asked, a quaver in his voice.

Before Alice had even finished nodding, the little foreman had disappeared into a side corridor. That was her chance! Alice spun and raced back into the castle, then hid behind a pillar when she heard footsteps approaching. They stopped just yards from her.

Peering around the edge of the column, she spotted Time fidgeting in front of a mirror. He was nervously patting his hair, trying to smooth it down. Then he cupped his hand in front of his mouth and exhaled into it, sniffing to check his breath. As he flicked imaginary dust off his cloak, a mournful note sounded through the castle, echoing off the walls.

Time rolled his eyes. "Ugh! Will this day never end?" He huffed in annoyance and turned on his heel.

Alice slipped quietly after him as he stalked into a room labeled UNDERLANDIANS LIVING.

The bright chamber was unlike anything Alice

had ever seen. Countless pocket watches hung from chains, their combined ticking filling the space like the buzzing of bees.

Walking among them, Time turned his face upward. "Who's stopped?" he asked. "Who has ticked their last tock? Tocked their last tick?"

He closed his eyes, his head cocked at an angle, as he listened carefully to the millions of pocket watches in his care.

"Ah," he said, opening his eyes. "Brilliam Hinkle!"

Time held out his hand and a chain dropped from above, depositing a watch into his palm.

"Yes, Brilliam Hinkle," Time confirmed as he glanced at the name engraved on the stopped watch. "Time's up." He snapped the watch closed without ceremony.

With a sympathetic frown, Alice imagined a man miles away, his heart abruptly giving out. How could Time be so cavalier about it? Had he been as heartless when he claimed the Hightopps? Her eyes narrowed as anger simmered inside her.

Oblivious to her glare, Time passed into a room labeled UNDERLANDIANS DECEASED. Cautiously, Alice poked her head around the door, wondering what she'd find. Unlike the last room, this one was deadly quiet. The sudden silence was almost as loud as a shout.

Time moved along an orderly row of pocket watches, reading out names from their backs as he went. "Higgens, Highbottom"—Time paused as he came to a gap in the watches, then shrugged and continued on—"Highview, Himmelby . . . ah, Hinkle."

With more gentleness than Alice had seen in him before, Time carefully hung the stopped watch in his hand on an empty chain in the row. He ran his fingers around its face and said softly, "I hope you used your time well. Good night."

Alice thawed slightly. Maybe he wasn't as cruel as she'd thought. Then the clicking of heels in the stone hall behind her made Alice spin in alarm. Shrinking back behind a column, she glanced at the floor, where a shadow loomed, coming ever closer. It was an odd shadow, though. She cocked her head as she studied it, trying to pin down what was wrong with it.

A bolt of fear shot through her as she realized the head was abnormally large. Only the Red Queen had a dome that misshapen! What was she doing there? Surely that wasn't who Time had been primping for, was it? Wasn't Iracebeth living in exile with her lackey, Stayne?

Once the footsteps had passed, Alice peeked around the pillar, her eyes widening in surprise at what she saw. Iracebeth's oversized head had, if anything, *grown* since Alice had last seen her. The Red Queen paraded down the hall as if she owned the place, Wilkins and a group of Seconds scuttling to keep up with her.

Turning a corner, the group left Alice alone once

again. She frowned, her mind spinning. Where the Red Queen went, trouble was sure to follow. Alice raced for the Chamber of the Grand Clock. If she was going to steal time, it was now or never.

Time hurried into his sitting room and rifled through a drawer. He lifted out a bottle of cologne—the one his darling preferred—and splashed some on. The cloying scent clogged up his nose and he coughed as he recapped the bottle and tucked it away.

An insistent knock sounded at the door and Time jolted upright. She was there!

"Coming, my love!" Time called, rushing to let his visitor in.

The Red Queen sauntered into the room, lifting one hand toward Time without even glancing at him. With a deep bow, he planted a servile kiss on her delicate skin.

"Oh, my radiant and beautiful dial-face, bulbous

of head and soft of heart," he said lovingly. "You are my only beacon!"

Iracebeth smiled at him indulgently; it was so nice to be adored. Thanks to her horrible sister, she no longer had a court full of nobles to compliment her. But Time helped soothe that wound. As she watched, he shuffled across the room to pick up a small music box and carried it back to her.

"Here," he said as he held it out gingerly. "A gift—nay, a tribute!"

Iracebeth's face lit up and her fingers twitched in excitement as she reached for it. "How sweet! Dear old tick-tock," she said. Who didn't love a good present?

As she turned the crank, a soft melody emerged, but the music box held—instead of a dancing ballerina or a kissing couple—a grim scene. Crouching with his head upon a block, a small mechanical king looked up at her as an executioner loomed over him. The executioner's ax swung down, neatly severing the king's head, which plopped into a basket in front of the block. When the song came to an end, the ax and head both inched back to their starting places.

Time gazed at Iracebeth anxiously. "I know how you love tiny things," he said, a hopeful note in his voice.

Clutching the music box to her chest, Iracebeth exclaimed, "I'll treasure it forever!" But only a second later, she tossed it to the side. Time winced as it thunked against the floor.

With a melodramatic sigh, the Red Queen twirled away, rolling her eyes skyward.

"Something troubling you, my dear?" Time asked.

Iracebeth cast him an appraising look, then sidled up to him, leaning in close to run her finger along his arm. "You know what I desire," she whispered. "With my big brain and your little Chronosphere, we could together rule the past, the present, *and* the future!"

Chapter Seven

At her words, Time's shoulders drooped. "But my dear, dear Iracebeth," he said. "I've told you time and again that's out of the question. You ask the impossible! You cannot change the past."

Iracebeth pulled away in disgust, the porcelain skin of her face turning a vibrant red. She *would* get her hands on that Chronosphere, no matter what it took. Then nobody—not her sister or any of Mirana's cronies—could stand in her way. She could finally right all the wrongs of the past and make sure the future went the way *she* wanted.

All of time would belong to her.

Alice found the Chamber of the Grand Clock abandoned, Wilkins and the Seconds most likely tending to another part of the castle . . . or to a demanding Red Queen. From the balcony, she gazed down at the clock, plotting her course. Cogs of all sizes spun in layers, clicking other pieces into place, turning wheels, winding belts, and swinging pendulums. At the center of it all, the silver light pulsed.

"The Chronosphere," Alice whispered, equal parts awe and determination in her voice.

She set off down the stairs and picked her way along a beam to her first challenge: a series of moving pendulums. She paused, and her eyes followed the closest one back and forth, back and forth as she judged the distance.

With a tremendous leap, she grasped hold of the pendulum. Wrapping her arms around the slippery metal, she let it carry her toward the next, then pushed off with her feet and spun in midair to catch the second pendulum. After a few more, she stopped to catch her breath.

The Chronosphere twinkled ahead, closer but still so far away. The sphere was spinning so fast its metal bands were a blur.

Creak. The door to the chamber opened and Time's Seconds filed into the room.

Alice froze, hoping they hadn't spotted her.

The Seconds whistled shrilly in alarm.

No such luck. In a clearly practiced maneuver, they clumped together, piling on top of one another in groups of sixty to form larger, more menacing figures.

"Seconds into Minutes," Alice observed before stepping off the last pendulum to the edge of a spinning wheel. There was no time to waste: with every passing second, the Minutes were adding up. And the Minutes moved smoothly through the clock, scaling the gears in acrobatic leaps.

Alice grabbed hold of a chain and rode it to a higher plane in the clockwork. That next level was a series of cogs, spinning in alternating directions. Beyond them, she could see the glowing sphere she needed, its light much brighter from there.

As the Minutes caught up to her, Alice hopped onto a cog and ran against its rotation until she could jump to the next.

The Minutes were right behind her. A few hasty Minutes got ahead of themselves, the spinning cogs flinging them into the air. Alice stayed focused on her task, looking ahead at an enormous revolving tube that led to the Chronosphere. There were always more Minutes in the day to catch her.

She gathered her muscles and launched herself into the tube.

Whump! Alice's feet slid out from under her. Like an out-of-control carousel, the tube whirled her around and around. As she tumbled upside down and then right side up again, she could see the Minutes converging on her—some from behind, some from ahead.

Trying to gain some traction, Alice spread her arms and legs wide, then somersaulted ahead of the tube's rotation and landed on her feet. She began running right away, keeping pace with the tube.

Thunk! Thunk! Thunk! Minutes landed on the outer edge of the tube above her.

Alice picked up speed, but the Minutes ran just as fast as she did, only in the opposite direction. They were at an impasse. She could not get away; nor could they get any closer.

"This is absurd," Alice muttered. She dug her feet in and stopped. Her abrupt shift in momentum threw the tube off. The Minutes flew into the air, shrieking in surprise.

Wiping her hands together, Alice calmly stepped out of the tube. She was close to her goal: she could see the Chronosphere glimmering ahead. But her heart sank as she saw the final obstacle.

Wham! A massive hammer slammed down in front of her, followed by several more. Somehow, she'd have to get through the pounding maze in one piece if she wanted to save her friend.

VIII

THE RED QUEEN'S temper was reaching a boiling point. What use was there in courting Time if he wouldn't bend the rules for her? Time was immensely powerful. That was why she'd started dating him in the first place. *The* only *reason, really,* she thought as she surveyed his elongated nose and bushy facial hair.

Now desperate, Time flung open the doors to a cabinet in his sitting room. It held his favorite treasures—things he had accumulated over the millennia. Everything from magic beans to dodo birds cluttered the shelves.

"My dear," Time said as he turned back to Iracebeth. "I would happily part with any one of my diversions." He gestured to the objects in the cabinet. One of the dodo birds let out a squawk and pecked at Time's hand.

Iracebeth huffed indignantly. She'd seen Time's little treasures before and they meant nothing to her.

"But I cannot give you the Chronosphere!" Time exclaimed.

"You would if you loved me," Iracebeth said sulkily.

"But I do love y—" Time's voice cut off abruptly as a shiver ran through his body. Looking down at his chest, his eyes filled with horror.

"The Grand Clock," he said. Without sparing a glance for Iracebeth, he raced from the room.

The Red Queen's eyebrows shot upward in surprise. Nobody ran out on her, not even Time. She clicked her tongue testily and hurried after him.

Chapter Eight

As Alice wavered at the edge of the giant hammers, one of the Minutes caught up to her and leapt ahead to guard the Chronosphere. But apparently even units of time could be off, and this one mistimed his jump. The round end of a hammer crashed down, splintering the Minute into Seconds, who sprinkled down between the clock's gears.

Alice shuddered. It was true: time would spare no man. Taking a deep breath, she danced forward, relying on her quick reflexes and memory of the hammers' pattern.

One step, wait, two, three, four, leap, leap, pause, seven, eight, jump!

Crack! She could hear the hammers smashing more Minutes into tiny fragments behind her. Alice pivoted through the final hammers and grabbed a piece of metal framework to steady herself.

Squeezed into a small gap between the hammers and the circular frame cradling the Chronosphere,

Alice swiftly patted herself over to make sure she was still in one piece. She let out a little sigh of relief, then faced the glowing orb.

Just then, Time rushed into the chamber, Iracebeth trailing him. Taking in the scene, he cried out in alarm and ran toward the Grand Clock.

Alice stretched up toward the shining Chronosphere. As her fingers drew near, it sparked and crackled fiercely. Biting her lip, she plunged her hand forward and clutched the Chronosphere. The small metal orb stopped spinning but continued to glow, its heat nearly burning her hand.

With a quick yank, Alice dislodged the Chronosphere and brought it to her chest. Separated from the Grand Clock, the orb began to cool down.

"No!" Time gasped, collapsing to his knees and clutching his chest.

Iracebeth peered at Time in irritation. "What's the matter with you?" she asked.

Time lifted a trembling hand, pointing at the

Grand Clock, where Alice was making her way back through the clockwork.

"The Chronosphere!" Time said frantically.

"Alice?" Iracebeth exclaimed. Her sister's pesky champion was the last person Iracebeth expected to see.

Oblivious to the new observers, Alice tucked the Chronosphere into her pocket and scrambled onto a beam. Behind her, the Minutes began to join hands, linking together to form a hulking mechanical beast.

"Cometh the Hour," Alice predicted as she picked up her speed.

The Hour ground toward her, its footsteps shaking the floor. As she glanced over her shoulder, her foot hit a spare part lying on the path. Alice arced through the air, then landed with a thump. At the impact, the Chronosphere rolled out of her pocket and bounced away.

Alice gasped and struggled to her feet while

the metal ball began to flash and expand. As the Chronosphere spun on its axis, its golden bands grew until the ball was the size of a carriage, with an open space visible between the rotating rings.

Whoosh! The Hour's massive arm swung through the air. Alice rolled to the side just in time. As she stood, she saw the Hour's hands reaching for the Chronosphere. Without thinking, she dove through the Chronosphere's whirling bands.

Inside, there were dials, levers, and several pulleys. Alice glanced around frantically. One of the chains was labeled PULL ME.

What else could she do?

Alice pulled it.

The Chronosphere lurched forward, its momentum pushing Alice against a metal arm.

"Ugh," Time moaned. "Why did I label that?"

Iracebeth glared at him in disgust as Alice and the Chronosphere careened out the door and into the hallways of the castle. The Hour lumbered after her, and Time and Iracebeth scrambled to catch up.

Once in the vast corridor, the Chronosphere crashed into columns left and right. Alice pulled on different levers and chains, trying to steer it as best she could. Glancing back, she saw the Hour charging at her.

Crossing her fingers, Alice slammed a lever, but instead of moving the Chronosphere forward, that propelled it *back* toward the Hour!

Boom! The Chronosphere smacked into the Hour, sending Minutes flying. *Aha!* Alice smiled triumphantly until she saw the Minutes swarming toward her again. She quickly pushed at levers and turned switches until the rings of the Chronosphere twirled faster, slicing through the air with a deafening whir. It was all Alice could do to cling to a handle, her body doubled over as the whole machine began to vibrate, screws threatening to pop off.

Time and Iracebeth rounded the corner to see the Minutes regrouping. But as soon as he saw the Chronosphere pulsing, Time knew it was too late. "No!" he cried out.

Poof! Alice and the Chronosphere disappeared.

IX

"WAIT! COME BACK!" Time shouted uselessly. He sank to his knees, head in his hands.

Fuming silently beside him, the Red Queen glared at the spot where Alice had been. That bothersome girl had taken *her* Chronosphere! Now her plans were ruined.

Time finally glanced up at her, then mumbled that he had to check on the Grand Clock and staggered away.

Inside the main chamber, Time studied the clock. The pendulums were still swinging, gears still turning. But he could feel a difference in their movement.

Iracebeth stalked in after him, her face a fiery red. "Alice?" She shrieked. "*The* Alice? The very reason I have been banished from my kingdom? She was here and you didn't think to *tell me*?"

Time cringed away from the Red Queen. "I—I . . . didn't realize," he stammered.

Stopping mere inches from his face, Iracebeth jutted her chin out, her hands clenched into fists at her sides.

"*Idiot! Imbecile!* You let Alice *steal the Chronosphere*!" She bellowed.

Time stumbled backward from the force of the Red Queen's breath. His hands drifted to his sideburns, worrying them into an even more absurd shape.

"I told her she couldn't have it," he said desperately. "She doesn't know what she's done."

Letting out a squeal of anger, Iracebeth spun

on her heel and stomped out of the chamber. She would have to come up with a new way to wreak vengeance on her sister and reclaim her rightful throne.

Normally, Time had all the time in the world. But for once he didn't have time to worry about his beloved. He felt a twinge in his chest. Time pulled open his vest and examined his heart clock; a small patch of rust had formed on the second hand.

Time paled. "It's happening already," he gasped. "Without the Chronosphere, the Grand Clock will unwind! Time myself will stop!"

He blinked rapidly, then shook his head. He could not let that happen. Avoiding it would mean stepping away from his post and leaving Wilkins in charge, but there was no way around it. Time himself had to travel back to stop Alice.

"Wilkins," he called. "Get in here! We've got a Tempus Fugit to build."

Prompt as ever, the small foreman bustled up,

carrying the spare clock parts and wood they would need to put together a basic time machine.

Time laid out all the pieces, then clapped his hands together. "Now then," he said. "This shouldn't take long."

In just one second—moving at warp speed as only Time could—they had fit together metal gears, wooden bars, and a narrow platform.

Once it was done, Time stepped back to admire the Tempus Fugit. A spring creaked ominously and one of the beams sagged in the middle.

"Splendid!" Time proclaimed. "Stand clear."

The wood groaned in protest as Time's weight hit the platform. Wilkins eyed the machine, wishing they had the Chronosphere instead; but then, if they did, they wouldn't be in that mess. As Time pumped a lever, the air began to waver around him.

"Now then, Wilkins!" Time barked. "You know how time works: goes forwards, not backwards, that sort of thing. Preferably in increments of one minute at a time."

"Yes, sir," Wilkins said. "I think I have the hang of it, after infinity."

"You must keep the Grand Clock ticking at all costs," Time continued. "Wish me luck, Wilkins. Now, where did that girl say she was heading?"

Time tugged on a pulley and the Tempus Fugit popped out of sight.

A ribbon of silvery light flowed around Alice and the Chronosphere, carrying them away from Time's castle.

Far below them, an ocean of moments swayed gently. Now that she could study the Chronosphere in peace, she had a better idea of how to maneuver it. It wasn't much different from navigating the *Wonder*. Alice felt a pang at the thought of her beloved ship. Would she ever sail it again?

Shaking off the depressing thought, Alice focused on her current problem—figuring out which way the past lay. With a light touch, she guided a lever forward, and the Chronosphere began to fly over the ocean.

Peering below, Alice spotted herself dangling from the second hand outside Time's castle and then plummeting toward the minute hand. Satisfied she'd found the right direction, Alice moved onward. Next she saw the White Queen and her friends clustered sadly around the table outside Marmoreal Castle. A much smaller Alice dropped into their midst.

"Whatever is the matter?" past Alice asked.

"The Hatter is the matter," McTwisp answered.

The Chronosphere whirled along, taking Alice away from the scene and backward in time. As the images blurred beneath her, faces and events zipping by, Alice began to worry. How was she going to find the right day? Then, on the horizon, she saw a flash of red and heard the nightmarish call of the Jabberwocky.

"Horunvendush Day," Alice whispered. It had to be. Tugging on a series of levers, Alice sent the Chronosphere diving toward the fateful day. The machine shuddered as it splashed through the barrier around the moment. When it hit the ground, Alice was tossed across the frame and out through the spinning rings.

Pfft. Alice spat out a mouthful of grass and raised her head. The Chronosphere, back to its regular, palm-sized form, rested a few feet away. She quickly swiped it from the ground, tucked it back in her pocket, and sat up to look around.

The remains of the Horunvendush field lay before her, smoke curling up from the blackened fairground. A stinging, sulfuric odor hung over everything. Ten yards away, Alice spotted a tall top hat, the fibers of its brim burning with embers. It was a bad sign. The Jabberwocky had clearly already made its attack.

Standing, she scanned the area for signs of life. Farther off, a figure with stooped shoulders was doing the same, his buoyant hair unmistakable.

"Hatter?" Alice called.

But the younger Hatter did not hear. He ran away, tears in his eyes, deaf to Alice's cries.

Before Alice could follow, hoofbeats pounded toward her, and she flung herself behind a bush just as Stayne, Iracebeth's enforcer, rode up. A heart-shaped eye patch covered one of his eyes, and the bloodred mark on his forehead stood out against his pale skin. In one hand he held a small sack, with something stirring inside. Clutched tightly in his other hand, the Vorpal sword was still shiny despite the ash-covered air.

Anger surged through Alice as she watched the despicable knight gallop up a hill to Iracebeth's side. Surveying the damage her Jabberwocky had done, the Red Queen smirked in satisfaction. She leaned over to kiss Stayne's cheek, and then they turned their horses and disappeared over the hill.

Alice desperately wanted to go after them and throttle the hateful Red Queen. But she wasn't there for Iracebeth. Dusting herself off, Alice walked to the center of the Horunvendush fairgrounds. They were completely abandoned, booths smoldering, the maypole cracked in half, and picnic tables flecked with ashes. Marking everywhere the Jabberwocky had breathed, charred lines of dirt slashed through the field, including the spot where Alice had seen the Hatter's family standing in Mirana's water-conjured image.

Despair stabbed through Alice. There was no way the Hightopps could have survived.

"Too late," she said, her fingers clenching her skirt tightly. "I was too late!"

There was nobody to hear, except for a lone tove.

The piglike animal slurped at the spilled liquid of a *pishsalver* barrel. As it trotted away, it began to shrink, but Alice was focused on a wink of blue she'd just noticed amid the devastation.

She picked her way to an old oak tree stump, then leaned her hand against a gnarled knot and peered inside a round hollow. Nestled within was the small blue hat, its paper miraculously unburned and a bright pink feather on its side fluttering cheerfully up at Alice.

"The blue hat!" Alice cried. Filled with renewed hope, she reached for it.

"I wouldn't do that if I were you," a voice warned.

Spinning, Alice saw Absolem, back in caterpillar form, lounging in a nearby tree.

"Absolem! You're the old you," she said.

"I'm always the old me," the Caterpillar replied haughtily. He gestured at the hat. "Wasn't this all explained to you before?"

Chapter Nine

Alice stood up and crossed to his tree. "I'll come back to Horunvendush Day once more and try again," she said.

Absolem sighed crossly and glared at her. "You can only visit each day once," he recited. "The consequences of seeing yourself would be catastrophic."

Her eyebrows furrowed, Alice pulled the Chronosphere from her pocket and studied it. "I could just go back to yesterday or the day before that and tell them not to come here at all."

"I fear, Alice, that you are failing to grasp the principles to which I am so assiduously alluding," Absolem said, his nose crinkling upward.

What is he talking about? Alice wondered. Before he could explain—if he would have chosen to at all, that is—an almighty sound ruptured the air. Alice's head snapped up and she saw a jagged tear appear in the sky. A wooden contraption flew through, Time at the helm.

Letting out a shout of outrage when he saw her, Time piloted his machine toward Alice.

"Give me what is mine!" he bellowed. "You have no conception of that in which you dabble!"

"Oh, dear," Absolem said flatly. "You seem to have upset somebody. You should probably go now."

Thank you for stating the obvious, Alice thought. But Absolem was right: if she wanted another chance at saving the Hightopps, she had to get away from Time. She flung the Chronosphere to the ground and leapt inside as soon as it expanded. With just a few tugs, she drove the Chronosphere up, up, up, and away.

X

BURSTING OUT of Horunvendush Day, Alice navigated the Chronosphere back into the rippling sky above the Ocean of Time. The Tempus Fugit, with Time at the wheel, popped out mere seconds later.

Time cranked his machine faster, gaining on her. Alice pulled on a lever, steering the Chronosphere to the left, but Time was too quick.

As he drew level with her, he shouted across the gap.

"You cannot win a race against Time! Give it

back. I am merciful," he wheezed between panting breaths. "But you must give it back!"

Glancing at Time, Alice noted that while his arms were a blur as he pumped the Tempus Fugit's levers, sweat beaded his forehead, and his chest heaved with exertion. It might be hard to outpace Time, but he seemed to be struggling.

She jerked the Chronosphere to the right and up in a single motion. She just needed to stay one step ahead of Time.

"Now where is yesterday?" Alice mused as she studied the ocean below. The images curled into endless waves and she couldn't pick out Horunvendush Day to find the next one back. "Oh, dear," she muttered.

Huffing and puffing, Time had managed to catch up. Alice swung the Chronosphere straight up, then looped behind the Tempus Fugit.

Time's shoulders slumped, his arms tiring as he looked back at her.

Chapter Ten

"You don't know what you've done!" he cried desperately.

Alice tugged on a pulley and the Chronosphere suddenly accelerated. *Oh, dear,* Alice thought. She hadn't meant to do that. But before she could steer it away, it bumped into the Tempus Fugit. With a tremendous clang, the two machines spun away from each other.

Throwing Alice sideways, the Chronosphere hurtled into the past. The golden sun pattern rippled across the floor. In the distance, Alice saw the glint of the Tempus Fugit, plummeting toward a different part of the ocean.

EEEEEEAAARRRROOOOM! The Chronosphere sliced into a day of the past, cutting through the air with a high-pitched shriek.

BOOM! As the sphere hit the ground and began to roll, the world spun for Alice. She caught glimpses of trees reaching downward and clouds drifting below her feet as she tumbled upside down. Finally, the Chronosphere bumped up against a rock and settled to a stop.

Feeling woozy, Alice stayed put, splayed out against the sphere's floor, until her vision—and stomach—adjusted. Once everything seemed normal again, she eased herself up onto her feet.

Alice stepped out of the Chronosphere, brushing herself off and automatically checking her father's pocket watch. The clock was still stopped, and added to that, a new crack ran down its face.

Sighing sadly, she dropped it back into her pocket along with the newly shrunken Chronosphere. She'd half hoped the watch would be ticking again, somehow a sign that she was back in a time when her father was alive. But maybe time—or Time, rather—didn't work that way.

Alice glanced around. She was standing on the outskirts of a quaint village that butted up against Tulgey Woods. Half the houses had thatched roofs, half were tiled, but all the buildings were askew in some way, as though their architects had found straight lines boring. Despite several houses' hanging over the street precariously, Alice had to admit that the end result was a cozy, whimsical town—much more appealing than the stuffy rectangular homes of London.

"Now where am I?" Alice mused. "And where are the Hightopps?"

Doo doo doo doooooooo! Trumpets blared in the distance. Curious, and with no other ideas as to where to look, Alice headed toward them. As she walked through the town, she saw that it had been decorated for some occasion, but whereas the Horunvendush Day celebration had taken place in a field, that day's festivities had taken over the streets. Strings of pennants fluttered from windows; stores had set up booths along the alleyways; and wagons of flowers had been rolled into a courtyard surrounding a statue of a king.

Ahead of her, a stream of people and creatures

was flowing over a bridge toward a red stone castle. Alice followed it and soon found herself in a gorgeous chamber with vaulted stone ceilings that reminded her of a cathedral. Sunlight poured in through arched windows along the right-hand wall and a massive stained glass window. Straight ahead, four figures sat on a raised platform.

Alice gasped. Mirana and Iracebeth made up half of the party on the stage. Their faces appeared much younger; they looked to be about Alice's age. Even more surprising, Iracebeth's head, while still larger than normal, wasn't quite as gargantuan as when Alice had first met her. Judging by their crowns, the two people sitting with them must be the sisters' parents—King Oleron and Queen Elsmere. Mirana had spoken of her parents only briefly, so Alice didn't know much about them beyond their names, but they both smiled pleasantly down at the gathered villagers.

Chapter Ten

Standing on tiptoe, Alice scanned the crowd for the Hightopps. She couldn't see their bright red hair anywhere. Movement onstage drew her eye and she realized with a start that the Hightopps, including Hatter, stood on the platform to one side of the royal family. Now all she had to do was stay close and wait for her chance to speak with them.

Alice made her way to the front of the crowd, watching as Zanik Hightopp crossed the stage to Mirana.

All around her, Underlandians clapped loudly as Zanik placed a delicate tiara on Mirana's head. Mirana, clad all in white, smiled sweetly at everyone. Per usual, Iracebeth's face was twisted in a scowl.

"And now," King Oleron announced, "the princess Iracebeth."

This must be some sort of coronation ceremony for the princesses, Alice thought. Zanik stepped to the side of the platform, where his son held out an oversized hatbox. Reaching in, Zanik carefully lifted an extra-wide tiara. Then he took his place behind Iracebeth and ceremoniously lowered it onto her head.

Except . . . it didn't fit.

Iracebeth's head was too large. As Zanik tried adjusting the angle of the tiara, the crowd around Alice murmured and the younger Hatter tried to stifle a snort of laughter.

"You are making me look foolish!" Iracebeth hissed at Zanik.

If the princess hadn't been so testy, Alice might have felt sorry for her. Hatter was caught up in the humor of the situation and couldn't help himself a second time: he giggled as his father struggled with Iracebeth's gigantic head.

"Get on with it!" Iracebeth burst out.

Doing his best, Zanik shoved the tiara down, but the force of his movement only snapped it in half. Jewels and pearls popped off and rolled down the steps of the platform, clattering loudly in the sudden silence. Several came to rest at Alice's feet and shimmered up at her.

After a few frozen moments, the assembled Underlandians began to titter.

"Old big 'ead broke her crown!" called someone from the audience.

As the laughter grew, Iracebeth's hands curled into fists and her cheeks flushed. Alice could see the tears brimming in the princess's eyes and she felt a twinge of sympathy. Being in front of a crowd could be nerve-racking enough; a crowd mocking you would be terrible.

"Silence!" Iracebeth bellowed. "The next person who laughs will never laugh again!" Alice's sympathy was quashed. That sounded like the Red Queen Alice knew—irrational and cutthroat.

"Iracebeth, please!" her mother interjected. "How could you ever stop people from laughing?"

Alice could think of a few ways the Red Queen

had done just that, but Queen Elsmere's concerned gaze seemed to subdue Iracebeth. The princess cast her eyes down to where red-hearted shoes peeked out from under her pink-and-black dress.

"Put a bag on her head!" someone else teased.

"If you can find one that would fit," another voice added.

The room exploded in laughter and Iracebeth shot to her feet, her whole body shaking in rage.

"Off with their tongues," she screamed. "Off with their ears! Off with their . . . heads! *Off with their heads!*" Flinging her arm forward, she pointed menacingly at the villagers.

Alice had heard the threat before, many times, but clearly the crowd hadn't. The Underlandians fell into a stunned silence.

With a frown, King Oleron rose from his throne. "Iracebeth, enough!" he snapped.

The princess froze, her arm still outstretched,

but she continued to glare at the crowd as her father approached.

Gently but firmly, the king took Iracebeth's arm and lowered it back to her side. Alice could see disappointment in his eyes as he addressed his daughter. "Iracebeth of Witzend. I had always hoped you would one day show the necessary qualities to become the queen you were born to be. I now realize, with a heavy heart, that day will never come."

"But, Father—" Iracebeth's voice cracked.

The king shook his head and faced the crowd. "People of Witzend, upon our passing, I hereby decree that my crown shall pass . . . to the princess Mirana."

In her seat, Mirana jolted in surprise, and the Underlandians fluttered at the announcement. As Iracebeth processed his words, her expression went from hurt to shocked and furious.

"But I'm the eldest! It's not fair!" she cried.

"You're dismissed," King Oleron said. He kept his eyes averted, as though his oldest daughter weren't there.

Iracebeth lashed out. "You always loved her best!"

"That's not true, Iracebeth," Queen Elsmere began, but the princess was too angry to listen.

"I hate you," Iracebeth spat. "I hate you all!"

Right there in front of Alice's eyes, Iracebeth's head began to expand, as though it were a balloon filling with air. Iracebeth grabbed her skull with her hands, then hurriedly stalked toward a stairwell next to the platform. Noticing the Hightopps, she paused.

"Zanik Hightopp," she said, her voice loaded with bitterness. "I will never forget what you and your family have done to me this day. Never."

Mirana rushed over and grabbed hold of her sister's arm.

Chapter Ten

"Iracebeth, please," Mirana said.

Iracebeth jerked away. "I'm not talking to you," she cried. "This is your fault. Everything is your fault!"

How could Iracebeth blame Mirana? Alice shook her head at the ridiculousness of it; none of this was Mirana's fault. Mirana hurried after her sister as Iracebeth stomped out of the room. The king and queen exchanged troubled looks and also retreated.

The coronation over, Underlandians began to funnel out of the castle. Alice pushed forward in the opposite direction, determined to reach the Hightopps. As she drew closer, she saw Zanik round on his son, his lips pressed together in a frown.

Hatter blinked innocently at him. "All I did was laugh, Father," he said. He held up his hands. "Her head is rather . . . voluminous! I couldn't help it."

"You cost the princess her crown," Zanik replied. "Do you know what this means for us?"

"Why am I never good enough for you?" Hatter asked.

"Why are you always such a disappointment to me?" Zanik said at the same time.

Hatter pulled back, quiet for a moment, and Alice found she was holding her breath. She knew what a parent's disapproval felt like.

"There," Hatter finally said, his voice surprisingly measured. "You've said it. Well, if I'm such a disappointment, I don't suppose you'll be sorry if I leave home."

"Tarrant, no!" his mother cried, rushing to stand between the men. "Please, Zanik, tell him to stay. Zanik!"

Zanik's mouth pulled into a flat line as his wife clung to Tarrant's sleeve. "If he is to be a hatter worthy of the Hightopp name, he must be sane, sober, disciplined, prudent, punctual, punctilious." He paused, regarding his son. "Everything he is now *not*!"

Alice winced on her friend's behalf. Zanik was wrong! She'd never met a better or more creative hatter than Tarrant. But the Hatter's lips only trembled slightly. He stiffened his back and gently disengaged from his mother's grip. With a quick nod, he whirled and marched out of the castle.

XI

IN THE WINDING streets of Witzend, people and creatures gathered in clusters to whisper about the results of the coronation. Keeping her eyes fixed on the lanky frame of the Hatter ahead of her, Alice wove through the groups.

"Excuse me?" she called. "Excuse me? Tarrant!"

Hatter spun, his face still tight with emotion. Alice pulled him into a hug, wanting to comfort him after that terrible exchange with his father. He was surprised, and his expression melted into bemusement.

"It's you, isn't it? It's really you!" Alice said, echoing what Hatter had once said to her.

"I'm sorry," Hatter replied. "Have we met?"

Alice stepped back, beaming up at him. "Yes! I mean, no. I mean, not yet. I'm Alice."

"Funny. I feel I should know you." Hatter's voice had returned to its usual quirky cadence.

"We met once," Alice explained. "When I was young."

"I'm afraid I don't recall," Hatter said.

Alice smiled. "Because it hasn't happened yet."

"When will it happen?"

"Years from now. When you're older," Alice answered.

Hatter cocked his head to the side. "I'll meet you when you're younger . . . and I'm older?"

"It doesn't make much sense, I know." Alice bit her lip as Hatter worked through the conundrum.

Suddenly, his face broke into the familiar grin

Alice had missed. "Of course it does!" he exclaimed. He started walking again, his steps more buoyant as Alice kept pace. "You're Alice—my new, old friend! You're bonkers, aren't you?"

"Am I?" Alice asked.

"All the best ones are," Hatter said, leaning in conspiratorially. He plucked a ribbon from one stall, then a purplemelon fruit from another. "You must meet my friend Thackery Earwicket!"

As they passed a crooked house, Hatter reached out and snatched a few tail feathers from a borogove bird perched on the windowsill. It let out a disgruntled squawk and fluttered away.

"He lives out by the old mill," Hatter continued. His fingers busily wove the ribbon around the fruit and feathers, attaching them to some fabric he'd pulled from his vest.

As the two of them exited the village and strode toward Tulgey Woods, Hatter drew a pair of scissors from a holster on his hip and snipped at the ribbon.

"I'm hoping he'll put me up for a bit," Hatter chattered on. "Will you join us for tea?"

Before Alice could answer, he whirled, presenting her with a stunning purple-and-blue hat he'd fashioned from the fruit, ribbon, fabric, and feathers. Delighted, Alice immediately placed it on her head. Hatter produced a hand mirror from one of his pockets and held it up with a flourish so she could admire herself.

"And the pièce de résistance," he said. Leaning forward, he tugged the ribbon on the hat. Immediately, its pink, white, and black feathers fanned out like a peacock's tail. Alice clapped her hands, impressed.

Linking arms, the two of them continued along the path until Hatter paused at an old oak tree with a hollow in its side.

"Can you keep a secret?" he whispered. Alice nodded and her friend's face became wistful. "This tree is magical," he said. "Every night when I was a boy, I would make a wish, and the next morning the tree would have granted it. Usually green-and-white Swizzles. Delicious! What a tree." He patted its bark gently before ambling onward.

Suddenly recognizing their surroundings, Alice pulled up short. They were close to the Horunvendush Day fairgrounds. She'd been so caught up in having her old friend back that she'd forgotten her mission.

"Wait! Stop!" she cried. "Your family is in danger. You must warn them about Horunvendush Day!"

Hatter regarded her blankly. "I've no idea what you're talking about," he finally said. "But if my father sent you to change my mind, you can tell him that I never will." He turned his back and walked purposefully away.

"Tarrant, wait!" Alice called desperately. "Listen! You are right now creating a past you will never be able to change! Hatter!"

But Hatter didn't turn around. His figure was soon swallowed by the shadows of the trees. Flinging up her arms in frustration, Alice headed back toward the village. Maybe the elder Hightopp would listen to reason.

She found Zanik Hightopp outside Witzend Castle, talking to a distraught Princess Mirana.

"I'm sorry, Mr. Hightopp," Mirana was saying as Alice approached. Her voice was sweet and sincere. "My sister wasn't always like this. But something happened when we were small."

Curious, Alice paused, waiting to hear more.

"It's fine, Your Majesty, really," Zanik said. He shifted on his feet, seemingly made uneasy by the fact that a princess was apologizing to him.

"It was Fell Day, many years ago," Mirana continued, oblivious to Zanik's discomfort. "It was snowing that night . . . she hit her head on a grandfather clock, in the town square." Mirana gestured toward the center of Witzend. Her eyes took on a faraway look. "Right at the stroke of six. I'll never forget."

An idea sprang to life in Alice's head. Not wanting to draw attention to herself, she slipped away quietly and headed out of town.

In Tulgey Woods the birds tweeted merrily and the sun shone down. But the Hatter didn't notice. He was slumped over the arm of a plump chair next to a series of tables that had been set up in a clearing. All his meager belongings were stacked nearby, just outside the house of his friend Thackery Earwicket.

Thackery, more widely known as the March

Hare, and Mallymkun, the brave little Dormouse, emerged from the house. Thackery balanced a tall stack of cups and saucers in one hand and waved a teapot in the other while Mallymkun carried a pile of silverware in her tiny hands.

"Teatime!" Thackery called brightly. The topmost cup began to slip off his tower, and he quickly swung his arm to shift everything back.

"Cheer up, Tarrant," Mallymkun said as she plunked down a spoon. Moving along the table, she set out another on the pristine tablecloth. "We'll have fun now that you're living here."

Hatter tried to shake off his gloominess; he didn't want to bring his friends down. He helped Thackery and Mallymkun lay out enough tea settings, cakes, scones, and sandwiches for a party of sixteen, even though it was just going to be the three of them—unless, of course, that delightfully strange Alice girl came along. Hatter felt bad for the way he had left things. It wasn't Alice's fault that his father disapproved of him. As Hatter turned to scan the trees for his new-old friend, a horrendous sound pierced the air.

From the sky, the Tempus Fugit whistled toward them. Time tried to steer his machine, but his arms were exhausted.

Boom! The Tempus Fugit crashed into the enormous sails of the windmill above Thackery's house.

The white fabric unfolded and the Tempus Fugit slid to the ground, bringing Time with it.

"Owwww," Time complained as the platform beneath him banged into the dirt. "Oooofff! Ughhhh," he moaned as a wooden beam thumped him on the head.

Speechless, Hatter, Thackery, and Mallymkun stared at the strange machine and the bushy-haired man crumpled in the grass.

Finally noticing them, Time scrambled to get out of the Tempus Fugit, his boots clanging against cogs as he pinwheeled his arms in a most undignified manner to get through the levers and switches.

Once he was finally free, he cleared his throat, then drew himself up to his full, imposing height. New wrinkles had formed in his forehead and there were bags under his eyes.

"Greetings," Time said. "I am Time. The Infinite and Immortal. You may express your awe and wonder." He peered down his nose at them. "But keep it short," he added, ever a stickler for himself.

Mallymkun bowed deeply, nudging Thackery with her elbow until he followed suit. Hatter merely tipped his head sideways to study the newcomer.

"I wonder, my lord," he said, "why you have lowered yourself to mingle amongst us mere and mundane mortals."

"Ah, well." Time's eyes shifted in his embarrassment. "I am looking for a girl called Alice. Have you seen her?"

Hatter pursed his lips, considering. Alice, he

liked, whereas this man seemed rather pompous. "What is your business with her?" he asked.

"She took something from me. I need it back as soon as possible," Time said.

Coming to a decision, Hatter smiled widely. "You're in luck, oh, Eternal One! Why, just today I invited Alice to tea. Have a seat. We can wait together." Hatter bowed, one arm extending toward the tea table.

Time strode past him and selected a tall armchair. As he settled in, Hatter caught Mallymkun's and Thackery's eyes over Time's head. He nodded slightly. *This will be fun,* Hatter thought.

He picked up a floral teapot—one of many teapots on the table—and poured some tea into Time's cup.

"If you're really Time itself, or himself, or whatever you are, perhaps you can answer me this," Hatter blathered on as he served their guest. "I've always wondered when 'soon' is." He set down the teapot only to snatch up a plate of scones and shove it into Time's face. "Is it before 'in a few minutes' or after 'a little while'?"

Time had to jerk backward to keep his nose clear of the pastries. Taking a moment to coldly study the Hatter, he clasped his hands.

"If you vex me, it'll be an eternity."

XII

YEARS FURTHER in the past, Alice steered the Chronosphere to a safe landing, which was much easier now that she wasn't being pursued. Once again, she stood on the outskirts of Witzend, but this time the air had a winter bite.

Her shoes crunched on the frost-covered ground as she made her way into the village. Strolling around her, people wore heavy coats, and their cheeks were pink from the chill.

Suddenly, a tiny grinning set of teeth, followed by an aqua-and-gray-striped kitten's tail, appeared from around a corner. *That must be a young Chessur!*

Alice thought. The tail twitched teasingly, and a bloodhound puppy—who could only be Bayard—bounded into sight. His paws just missed the tail as kitten Chess whisked it away.

Puppy Bayard's feet skidded out from under him on the icy ground, and he went sprawling. Chess giggled gleefully. Two plump young boys toddled into view, their arms knocking against each other; these were the young Tweedles! Trailing behind them was a very dapperly dressed eight-year-old boy with bright orange hair. There was no mistaking the Hatter, no matter his age. His green plaid coat swung open to reveal a light pink necktie tucked into his vest, and his ensemble was completed by a red velvet top hat.

Smiling, Alice watched her young friends. Chess was now leading Bayard on a merry chase through the crowd while the Tweedles bounced off people's legs as they tried to keep up. The bright blue laces of Hatter's boots flopped cheerfully as he danced after them.

"Tarrant!" A stern voice called.

Hatter stopped mid-step and turned toward his father, whose tall figure was framed by the doorway of his shop. Zanik, his arms crossed over his chest, was frowning.

With a sheepish grin, Chessur melted into the air, then reappeared farther down an alleyway. Bayard and the Tweedles hurried after him without a backward glance at Hatter.

Dragging his shoes along the cobblestones, the young Hatter trudged toward his family's shop. He perked up when he noticed Alice standing in the shadows. Perhaps drawn by her colorful tunic or the hat on her head that he himself would later create, he skipped over to her. Grabbing her hand, he pulled her into the shop.

Inside, the small space was cluttered with the

tools of the trade. Hung around the top of the room like a border of wallpaper, hats of all shapes and colors beckoned to customers. Cabinets of threads and ribbons were tucked against the far wall, and hat stands and mirrors stood waiting near the door. At the back, beyond everything, Alice saw a staircase, which she guessed led up to the family's living quarters.

Zanik, who had his nose buried in an account book, glanced up, his eyes briefly focusing on Alice.

"We're closed," he said.

Hatter ran around the desk to join his father.

"Papa! Look!" he cried. "A customer with a lovely head. Right here!"

"I'm sorry, miss," Zanik continued, ignoring his son. "You'll have to come back another time."

Zanik shut the ledger with a snap, tucked it under his arm, and moved toward a back room. Alice knew he wanted her to leave, but she stayed put, waiting for an opportunity to broach the subject of the future with Zanik now that she was there.

"Oh, and, Papa, look!" Hatter clamored at Zanik's side, tugging on his coat.

"Not now, Son," Zanik said firmly.

"I made something for you in school," Hatter continued. He flopped open his schoolbag and dug into it.

Zanik sighed. "I keep telling you I'm busy. What is it?"

Caught up in their conversation, both Zanik and Tarrant seemed unaware that Alice had lingered in the shop.

Hatter pulled out his present, his face full of hope. Alice felt a jolt, her heart fluttering at the sight of the tiny blue paper hat cupped in his hand.

"A hat!" Hatter exclaimed as he held it out proudly.

"This? Let me have a look." Zanik took the hat

and began to examine it. "If my son is going to make a hat, he will make a proper one. Do something, do it right, eh? Look here"—he jabbed at the hat—"the band is crooked."

As Zanik's fingers poked at the band, the paper ripped. In the stillness of the shop, the sound echoed. Alice cringed; Hatter looked like he'd been slapped.

"Ah. Oh. Hmm," Zanik muttered. "Well, cheap materials. There's your lesson. Tell you what, tomorrow I'll help you make a real hat, Son. Not one of these pretend ones, eh?"

Zanik balled up the paper hat and tossed it into the waste bin. Hatter's eyes brimmed with tears as he saw it arc through the air. Fleeing from the room, he passed his mother on the stairs. Though Tyva reached for him, he barreled past her without a word.

"You're too hard on him, Zanik," Tyva said as

she joined her husband. She did not notice Alice by the door, either.

"I'm hard on him because he has great potential." Zanik's mouth twitched slightly. "It's how my father was with me, and his father with him."

He walked to his desk and opened one of the drawers. Inside, Alice saw a sea of green-and-white Swizzles. She stepped forward slightly to make sure she wasn't imagining things. The movement caught Zanik's eye, and his head snapped up. With a quick push, he shut the drawer.

"Miss, I told you, we're closed," Zanik said in a tone that brooked no argument.

Alice bowed her head and backed out of the store, her expression pensive.

Time shifted irritably in his chair. Alice still hadn't shown up for tea and the Hatter was becoming tiresome—as were his companions. Time's eyes drifted to where Mallymkun danced in circles on the table and the March Hare bounced up and down as he poured himself some tea.

Leaning far too close, Hatter continued babbling. "I mean, are you really who you say you are?" he asked. "Or do you exist at all? Some say Time is an illusion." Hatter reached forward to poke Time's face.

Time swatted Hatter's hand away. "I am not an illusion!" he snapped. "Could an illusion do this?"

Time ripped open his cloak and vest and grabbed hold of the second hand of his heart clock, forcing it still. Instantly, the world froze. The Dormouse balanced on one foot and the stream of tea from Thackery's pot looked like a ribbon, its edge stopped above the cup.

Hatter patted his chest to make sure he was still able to move, then studied his two friends. He stooped to peer closely at the tea.

"Actually quite impressive," Hatter admitted.

Time let go of the second hand and everything lurched back into motion . . . including the tea.

Sploosh! The liquid splashed down onto Hatter's face. Blinking rapidly, he straightened up, tea dripping from his eyebrows.

Time's breaths came in heavy pants and his shoulders sagged slightly. "*Now*, when is Alice coming?" he asked impatiently.

Hatter's lips twitched. Imagine Time's not knowing the *when* of something. Surely this all-powerful being would be aware of every event in every second. Time might be easier to fool than he'd thought.

Hatter sprang around Time's chair, leaning over one shoulder, then the other as he fired questions.

"Is it true you heal all wounds? Do you fly when you're having fun? And why is it you wait for no man?" His voice rippled with a manic energy.

"We have such a lovely Time here!" Mallymkun cried, rocking back in laughter.

"The best Time ever!" Thackery said, joining in the fun.

Pausing behind Time's chair, Hatter reached down, his fingers delving into the tufts of hair on either side of Time's face. "Look!" Hatter giggled. "I've got Time on my hands!"

Mallymkun leapt over a teacup and slid up next to them. "Yes, but Time is on my side," she crowed.

"Oh, oh!" Thackery rushed around the table, a teapot wobbling in his hands. "Now I'm serving Time!" The March Hare's ears flopped forward as he bent to pour tea into Time's already full cup.

"I'm racing against Time!" Hatter shouted, running in place next to Time's chair. "I'm passing Time!" He zoomed away.

Thackery giggled.

"I'm beating Time! I'm killing Time," Mallymkun said, banging her fists on Time's shoulder.

"I'm saving Time," Hatter countered, plucking the Dormouse off their guest.

"I'm losing Time!" Mallymkun stretched out her hands as Hatter carried her away, then dropped her onto the table.

Hatter circled back, then popped up behind Time's chair again and grabbed his arms. "Look, look," he cried. "Time is flying!" He flapped Time's arms up and down.

Thackery and Mallymkun doubled over in laughter.

"No, no, wait!" Hatter said. "Time is crawling. C . . . r . . . a . . . w . . . l . . . i . . . n . . . g!" He wheeled Time's arms slowly through the air.

"Enough!" Time bellowed. Flinging the Hatter off, he jerked to his feet and, with narrowed eyes, rounded on him. "She's not coming, is she?"

"I never said she was, old bean," Hatter said nonchalantly. He sauntered to a chair and slid into it. "I merely said I *invited* her."

Time's eyes nearly popped out of his skull. "What? You! You—you . . ." he stammered in rage. He took a deep breath, then continued more calmly. "Nicely done, sir. But now it's my turn." His eyes glinted menacingly. "You were asking when 'now' is?"

Time lifted his cloak once again to reveal the clock in his chest. The hands read 5:59.

"Now is precisely one minute to teatime," Time continued. "And until young Alice eventually joins you for tea, it will *always* be one minute to teatime." He smiled smugly. "Enjoy your little party."

Spinning the clock in his chest backward, Time disappeared.

Hatter tried to stand up but couldn't! He pushed his arms down harder on the chair's arms and strained with his legs, but it was no use.

He was stuck in place.

"What? Wait, what's he done?" Mallymkun asked. She and Thackery both twisted in their own seats, squirming to get free.

Chapter Twelve

"The blighter's stuck us all at one minute to teatime!" Hatter slumped back in his chair. "Slurkingsluvishurksum!" he swore softly. That had not gone as expected.

XIII

FURTHER IN THE PAST, a young Queen Elsmere was elbow-deep in flour as she rolled dough in the Witzend Castle kitchen. Normally, she loved baking—she found a certain tranquility in the act—but at the moment, the queen was feeling far from peaceful. At the table behind her, her six-year-old daughters squabbled as they tugged back and forth on an almost empty plate of tarts.

"You're eating all the tarts!" Mirana complained.

"You can have the crusts," Iracebeth said, licking berry juice off her fingers.

Huffing in annoyance, Queen Elsmere spun toward them. "If you can't get along, there will be no more tarts for either of you," she declared. "Now out of my kitchen. Scat!" She shooed them away with her rolling pin.

Reluctantly, the girls slid off the bench and headed for the door. With one last longing look over her shoulder, Mirana followed her sister out of the room.

Then she paused, watching Iracebeth trudge away in the other direction. Her sister was most likely going off to play with her ant farm. Mirana waited until she was out of sight.

Cautiously, Mirana turned around, poking her head through the doorway they had just exited to scan the kitchen. Queen Elsmere bustled around, chopping vegetables for dinner and tossing them into a large pot on the hearth. Her mother must have sent their cook home for the night. She did that whenever she wanted the kitchen to herself to calm her nerves. Mirana hesitated, knowing her mother was already in a bad mood. But the plate of tarts was practically calling to her. And she never got the juicy berry parts with Iracebeth around.

When Queen Elsmere turned her back to the door to wash some carrots at the sink, the princess seized her chance. She darted across the stone floor, snatched the tarts, then whirled back through the doorway as her mother spun around.

Queen Elsmere shook her head as she spotted the empty plate. "I told them . . ." she muttered.

With light steps, Mirana dashed up the spiral staircase to the tower bedroom she shared with Iracebeth, shoving the tarts into her mouth as she went. Ducking into the circular room (her half decorated in white, Iracebeth's half decorated in red), she gobbled up the last tart, its tangy sweetness filling her mouth. She sighed happily.

Footsteps sounded in the hall and Mirana looked around in a panic. Burying a twinge of guilt, Mirana quickly swept the crusts onto the floor and under the bed on Iracebeth's side. As the door creaked open, Mirana straightened, her hands clenched behind her back.

Iracebeth walked in, carefully balancing a jar of ants. She stopped and peered at her sister suspiciously. Mirana was standing on Iracebeth's side of the room and had a shifty look on her face.

"What are you doing?" Iracebeth asked.

"Nothing," Mirana said. Sliding past her sister, she raced out the door.

Iracebeth shrugged and continued into the room. When she got to her side, she flicked open the ant farm on her nightstand and slowly poured the ants in.

"Here you are!" Iracebeth trilled to them. "A nice new home. I hope we'll be friends."

As she bent to watch the ants settle in, she

noticed a speck on the floor by her bed. She peered closer. Was that a tart crumb?

The door creaked open and her mother strode in, Mirana in tow.

"What did I tell you?" Queen Elsmere's voice was sharp as she faced her daughters. "No more tarts!"

"I didn't eat any tarts!" Iracebeth protested.

Elsmere's gaze landed on the floor. "Why are these crusts under your bed?" she asked.

Iracebeth's eyes widened as she pieced the truth together: *she* hadn't eaten any tarts in there, but Mirana had been on her side of the room. . . . Her chest aching at the betrayal, she pointed at her sister. "She put them there!"

Elsmere turned to face Mirana. "Did you, Mirana?"

Mirana's face was pale and she shrank back from them.

"You did! Tell her," Iracebeth insisted. Mirana

had stolen the tarts, so Mirana should be the one in trouble.

"Tell the truth, Mirana," Elsmere said. "Did you eat the tarts and put the crusts there?"

Mirana's lips trembled. She couldn't bear it when her mother was mad at her. "No," she said. Her voice was small and wavered slightly, but then she looked up at the queen, her face sweet and innocent.

Iracebeth's jaw dropped. "But you did! You're lying," she cried. How could her sister do this to her?

Elsmere had heard enough. "The tarts are under your bed," she said to Iracebeth. "Don't blame your sister. She's innocent."

"No! It's not fair!" Iracebeth stamped her foot.

Elsmere reached for her daughter's arm, but Iracebeth dodged away and fled down the hall, sobbing.

—

Chapter Thirteen

Gong! In the town square, Alice stopped at the sound. Snowflakes landed on her eyelashes as she stared up at the clock tower.

"The stroke of six!" Alice exclaimed. She looked around frantically, hoping to spot Iracebeth, but there were no little princesses in sight.

The only creatures in the square were a fish gentleman in a top hat, who was holding an umbrella to ward off the snow, and two frog men in delivery uniforms, carrying a grandfather clock.

Gong!

There! A young girl of maybe six or seven years old hurtled down the street, tears streaming from her eyes. Her head was unremarkable, perfectly normal in size, but Alice recognized Iracebeth's heart-shaped face and pouty lips. She *had* been normal once upon a time.

Gong!

"The clock! She'll bump her head," Alice cried. She had to stop it!

Diving forward, Alice knocked a frog deliveryman to the ground. One end of the clock thunked down on the street.

"Oi, what—" the frog man yelled.

Gong!

Alice sat up triumphantly, oblivious to the frog's complaints. But Iracebeth was still running blindly into the square. The young princess now avoided the frog men, but the gentleman fish was directly in her path.

"Careful, miss!" the fish spluttered.

Gong!

Swerving too sharply, Iracebeth slipped on the snowy cobblestones and flew toward her father's statue at the center of the square.

"No, no, no!" Alice cried.

Gong! Iracebeth slammed into the base of the statue. Several white rosebushes around the statue, which were already bent under the snow, rained petals on the princess.

With a pitiful whimper, Iracebeth sat up slowly, her hands alternately cradling her head and swatting away roses.

"My head!" she wailed. "Oh, my head, my head! Stupid roses!"

The frog men and gentleman fish rushed over.

"Is your head all right, miss?" a frog man asked.

"Careful, it's swelling up!" The fish gasped.

Alice stepped back under an awning. There was nothing she could do. She'd failed . . . again. Iracebeth's skull puffed out and tears poured down her face. King Oleron and Queen Elsmere ran into the square and immediately knelt at their daughter's side. Princess Mirana followed them, her eyes wide.

A tear rolled down Alice's cheek as she watched King Oleron lift little Iracebeth into his arms. Walking beside them back to the castle, Queen Elsmere held Iracebeth's hand and murmured reassurances. Mirana trailed after them, guilt written across her face.

"You cannot change the past," Alice whispered sadly. As she turned away, she noticed the window of Hightopp's hat shop glowing.

Inside, she could see Zanik bending down. He stood back up, a crumpled blue paper hat in his hands. Smoothing the paper out, he ran his fingers along the feather, a smile on his face. Then he tucked the hat into his breast pocket, right above his heart.

Alice froze, remembering the rest of Time's reprimand: *Although, I daresay, you might learn something from it. . . .*

"He kept it," Alice gasped.

Memories whirled through her head.

Time's room of Underlandians Deceased—Higgens, Highbottom, Highview . . . *There were no Hightopps on file!*

A furious Iracebeth threatening vengeance on Zanik at her failed coronation.

A hopeful young Hatter holding up a paper hat to his father.

Zanik's secret stash of green-and-white candy—the very same candy Hatter would get from his favorite tree.

And finally, the blue paper hat hidden inside the trunk of the same tree, the ground outside charred but the paper hat untouched.

"They're alive. They're *alive*!" Alice cried happily. Zanik must have hidden the paper hat he'd kept for all those years in the tree to give his son a sign that they were alive! Hatter was right! She twirled with joy.

"Oof!" Alice smacked into Time. He was dusted in snow, and his eyebrows were drawn so close together that they looked like one long white caterpillar.

Latching on to her with a clawlike grip, he hauled her into the nearest shop, which happened to be a clockmaker's.

The place was dark and abandoned but for the hundreds of chiming clocks hanging on the walls and resting on shelves. They came in all shapes and sizes, some hammered from metal, others carved out of wood. In the light streaming in through the window, Alice could see deep crags in Time's face. He looked like he'd aged twenty years since she'd last seen him.

"You have no idea how reckless you have been! The dangers you have courted!" Time shook her arm as he spoke. "If I hadn't caught you—"

His eyes bulged slightly and he paused to gasp for breath. Letting go of her, he clutched at his chest.

The clocks in the shop all stopped mid-tick and Alice was caught in a bubble—frozen. Only this wasn't Time's doing. The clock shop's walls pushed outward, then contracted with a snap and continued to press inward. As Time swung his head to look around, his body moved at a fraction of the speed it usually did. A bolt of panic ran through him. The clocks in the shop all began to chime and whirl—some moving forward, others backward.

Chapter Thirteen

All at once, everything went back to normal. But Time knew the trouble wasn't over. The Grand Clock itself must be rusting. While Wilkins and the Seconds might have bought Time some more of himself, they couldn't save him completely. As Alice watched, he pulled open his vest and stared in alarm at the spreading rust on his heart clock.

"I need that Chronosphere—now!" Time cried. His voice was thin and shaky as he advanced on Alice.

"Let me go," Alice pleaded. She finally had the pieces she needed to save her friend's family. "The Hightopps! I know where they are. I'm going to rescue the Hightopps!"

"You'll rescue no one," Time wheezed. "There is nowhere you can go that I won't find you."

Backing away, Alice bumped into a cabinet and slid sideways, glancing behind her as she went. There, on the wall above a fireplace, hung a large antique mirror. The glass seemed opaque, its center turning into wisps of mist.

"My dear." Time chuckled as Alice clambered up onto the mantelpiece. "You cannot escape Time."

"Actually," Alice said as Time reached for the Chronosphere, "I can." Confidently, she stepped backward into the mirror.

Time lunged forward, but his fingers grasped nothing but air as Alice disappeared into the mist. Feeling a jolt, Alice could see the outline of the Ascots' parlor room. Then *bam*. She thumped her head against something terribly hard. *I don't seem to be doing a good job preventing head trauma this evening*, Alice thought before everything went black.

XIV

A BRIGHT LIGHT woke Alice. She cracked her eyes open, raising her hand to shield them. Above her loomed a plain white ceiling she'd never seen before. Feeling a bit dizzy, she sat up slowly.

She was lying in a metal-framed bed. The room was shaped in a peculiar circle and filled with other beds, all of them empty. A box with wires coming out of it sat next to a hulking bathtub, and across the room, a man in a white doctor's coat stood in front of a washbasin mirror, smoothing his hair.

Fabric rustled and Alice turned to see her mother in a chair by her side.

A creeping suspicion snuck into Alice's mind. Where had her mother brought her? This place was strange and oddly menacing. Surely she hadn't locked her up in an asylum . . . had she?

Drifting up to the sides of her head, Alice's fingers patted half frantically at the strands of her hair. They were shorter than they should have been—much shorter. Someone had cut her hair while she'd slept.

"Where am I?" Alice asked. "How long have I been here?"

"Not long," her mother said reassuringly. "You were in an upstairs room at the Ascots. Perhaps you fainted?"

"No," Alice said. She hadn't fainted; she was sure of that. She was not the fainting sort.

Helen darted a glance at the doctor, who was

approaching, then lowered her voice. "They say you were trying to get under the furniture. Talking about the atmosphere?" Her eyes looked worried.

"The Chronosphere," the doctor clarified, peering at his notes.

"The Chronosphere!" Alice began patting her clothes. She was wearing a rough beige tunic and a pair of thin pants made from the same material. The sphere was gone. "I have to get it back and save the Hightopps before the end of Time!"

"Let's see," the doctor said, marking things down on his clipboard. "Excitable, emotional, prone to fantasy—a textbook case of female hysteria."

Alice glared at him, but Helen ignored the doctor and brought her face close to Alice's. Brushing her hand over Alice's cheek, she spoke soothingly. "Alice, please," she said. "You've had a long voyage and you're exhausted. We can all agree to that."

Just beyond her mother's head, Alice spotted a

table laid out with medical tools. A gigantic syringe filled with golden liquid gleamed ominously at her. Throwing back the sheets, Alice started to leap from the bed. Her mother backed away hurriedly, but the doctor's arm snapped out like a bar across Alice's chest. His hands clamped on her shoulders and he pushed her back down to the mattress.

Watching her daughter squirm under the doctor's weight, Helen shifted uncomfortably. "Dr. Bennet, is it necessary to—" Helen began timidly.

"Excuse us, Mrs. Kingsleigh," Dr. Bennet interrupted. "What Alice needs right now is a long, dreamless sleep." He nodded to two orderlies who had just entered.

Furious, Alice lashed out with her legs, kicking anything she could reach.

"Now, now, Alice," Dr. Bennet said. "You mustn't be so headstrong."

Helen started slightly; she'd often said those

very words, but hearing someone else utter them cast everything in a new light.

The orderlies reached Helen's side, and their hands gently guided her toward the door. She obeyed reluctantly, staring back over her shoulder at her struggling daughter as though she wasn't sure she was doing the right thing.

As Dr. Bennet lifted his eyes to watch them leave, Alice's hand snaked out to the side, then quickly back. The door swung shut behind her mother, and Dr. Bennet turned toward his tools.

"That's odd," he muttered. "Where did I put the nee—"

Springing up, Alice plunged the needle into the doctor's back. She injected the golden liquid, then leapt out of the way as he slumped toward the floor. Whatever it was, it was fast-acting and powerful.

"Oi!" An orderly shouted as he came back into the room. He and his partner raced toward her.

Alice crouched and snatched the key ring from Dr. Bennet's side. Her eyes landed on her father's pocket watch, which the doctor must have confiscated, among the tools. Grabbing that, too, Alice vaulted over the next bed as the orderlies pounded near. She shoved through the door and out into the main hallway.

Rushing out after her, the men shouted to their colleagues. More orderlies poured into the hallway from the other direction and Alice skidded to a stop, the soles of her shoes sliding on the wooden floorboards. She pivoted sharply and barreled up a stairwell, taking the steps two at a time. At the top, she heard music coming from behind a set of double doors.

As she weighed her options, Alice glanced down the stairwell. The orderlies were panting as they jogged toward her. Quickly, she ducked through the doors and found herself surrounded by a soothing harmony.

Chapter Fourteen

The room was large and windowless. Fifty or so patients sat on stiff wooden chairs, facing the front, where a string quartet played for them. Slouched against the wall, a bored orderly had his back to her.

Alice slid into a row, excusing herself to the people she passed. They gazed blankly up at her as she made her way to an empty seat. Just as the doors swung inward and a very out-of-breath group of orderlies tramped in, Alice slipped onto the chair. Out of the corner of her eye, Alice watched as they split up and began searching the crowd.

"Alice?" a soft voice asked.

The song came to an end and Alice recognized her own aunt sitting in front of her. What was she doing there?

"Aunt Imogene!" Alice said in surprise.

Her aunt twisted in her seat, her kind face full of hope. "Have you seen my fiancé?"

Alice shook her head sadly. Poor Aunt Imogene.

Alice couldn't believe her relatives had locked up her aunt just because she had an imaginary romance. It was perfectly harmless! Evidently her family couldn't cope with any women who had imagination.

The musicians' bows sliced across their instruments as the next song started. With a covert sideways glance, Alice noticed an orderly spot her and start gesturing at his partner. Together, they waded through the patients toward her.

"He's a prince, you know," Aunt Imogene continued blissfully. "He's coming to get me. All I need to do is wait."

Alice leaned forward and pressed the set of keys into her aunt's hands, gazing into her eyes intently.

"Don't wait any longer, Aunt Imogene," she whispered. As she knew all too well, you had to make the most of your time. Alice sprang to her feet and darted down the row away from the orderlies.

With a shout, they surged forward, but Alice was

already out of the room through another door and climbing up a narrow staircase.

At the top, Alice emerged on the asylum's roof. The London sky was pink and purple, the sun just dipping below the horizon. A Union Jack flapped in the evening wind, and the air reeked of factory smoke. Wasting no time, she picked her way around the metal pipes to the edge of the roof and leaned over.

Dangling toward a broad courtyard below, a metal ladder was attached to the bricks. But there would be no escape that way; several orderlies were already climbing it.

One of them spotted her and began pulling himself up faster, shouting at the others to hurry. Alice backed away and scanned the roof again. There had to be another way out.

Just then, the door she'd come through was flung open and the other set of orderlies tumbled onto the rooftop. Alice darted toward the flagpole, a crazy plan in her head.

She grabbed the rope and wrapped one end around her waist, her fingers moving rapidly.

"If three years at sea taught me anything," she muttered to herself, securing the other end to the base of the flagpole, "it was how to tie a bloody good knot!"

Alice spared a glance at the advancing orderlies as she gathered up the slack in the rope; then she spun and leapt off the roof.

For a second, she hung in midair, the world almost—but not quite—frozen in time. Then, twisting to face the building, she braced herself for impact.

Her feet slammed against the bricks and she pushed off again, letting out more slack in the rope. Below her, an empty carriage waited outside the asylum. With a few more leaps, Alice was within range. Jumping down into the open carriage, she landed with a thud on the cloth seat.

Chapter Fourteen

The horses whinnied in alarm and jolted forward. Alice had to move fast to scramble up into the driver's seat, untying the rope from her waist as she went.

"Oi!" The carriage driver raced out from the building, waving frantically at her. "You can't take that!"

As she gathered up the reins, Alice turned to wave at him apologetically. "Sorry. Needs must," she called. "I plead insanity!"

Feeling wild and free, she galloped the horses through the institution's gate and into the night. Alice didn't recognize any of the streets around the asylum, but she heard Big Ben tolling in the distance and used the bell's chime to veer north. Soon she came to more familiar neighborhoods, but instead of heading for home (there was no point in that; her mother would just send her back to the asylum, and she had a mission to complete), Alice steered the horses toward the countryside.

There was hardly anyone else on the roads, and Alice passed unnoticed through the moonlit landscape. The wind ruffled what was left of her hair as she finally pulled the carriage to a stop outside the drive to the Ascots' mansion. After climbing down, she clucked to the horses, sending them back toward the center of London. They'd find their way home.

Silently, Alice made her way along the path. No movement came from within the Ascot mansion, everyone inside surely fast asleep at that hour. She circled the building until she found a window that had been left ajar.

With a strong push, she hefted the pane higher, and she wriggled her way up and through, landing in a disheveled heap on a couch just under the window. Sitting up, she recognized the library. Books were stacked on top of every available surface—including assorted tables and cabinets—and large family portraits hung on the walls. Hamish gazed down disapprovingly at her from one, the artist having perfectly captured his stiff and superior posture. Ignoring him, Alice strode to the oak door and tugged.

It didn't budge.

She tried again, throwing her weight backward and gripping the knob with both hands.

Nothing.

Creak. Alice froze at a noise behind her. As she turned slowly, her heart sank.

Across the room, James Harcourt sat at a desk, pen in hand. There were books piled all around him, as though he had built himself a mini fort. His eyebrows were raised in surprise as he studied her. He slowly got to his feet and edged past a piano toward her.

Alice backed away. "Please," she whispered desperately.

Stopping in front of the door, James lightly pushed against it. The door inched open as he stepped back, smiling.

"It's easier if you push," he said.

"Thank you!" Alice's shoulders relaxed.

"They're going to ask your mother to sign over the ship. Seeing's you're so unwell," James added as Alice moved toward the door.

"Buy me some time?" she asked.

He nodded and Alice shot him a smile before ducking out the door and heading upstairs.

In the dusty parlor, Alice dropped to the floor, searching frantically along the Persian rug and under the chairs. Her heart raced. *Where is it?*

Then something twinkled under the sideboard. *There!*

Alice lunged toward it. Wrapping her fingers around the Chronosphere, she brought it to her chest with relief. As she stood, the looking glass shifted, the silver mist swirling once again within the frame.

Newly determined, Alice climbed up onto the mantelpiece, a fierce look in her eyes. With the Chronosphere in one hand and her father's pocket watch in the other, she stepped through the looking glass one more time.

XV

IRACEBETH PACED along the balcony of her castle deep in the Outlands. It was nowhere near as comfortable as her previous palace, and the walls smelled of mildew—an unfortunate side effect of being banished to the Outlands and having only vegetable and plant matter as building materials. Iracebeth sniffed unhappily, lifting her binoculars to her eyes and scanning the horizon.

There was nothing but rocks and grasslands for miles. Cursing her sister for exiling her to this awful place, Iracebeth whirled and stalked inside, the skirt of her dress swishing through the air.

Maybe Time had some news that would cheer her up. Surely by now he'd tracked down Alice and retrieved the Chronosphere. She paused in a hallway to peer into a dark void.

"Tick-tock?" she called. *"Tick-tock!"* There was no answer. "Where is that old fool?" she muttered as she continued on to her private chamber.

The walls and ceiling, like everything else in her castle, were formed from bloodred trees and vines. The bed was draped in red blankets, and a threadbare canopy drooped over the top of it. All around the room, the vegetables that had refused to bow to her will hung from spikes or were stretched out on racks. Jars of mushrooms, mandrake, and other useful sources of poison cluttered her bookshelf, and a desk sat to one side, covered with her sketches of the Chronosphere and how to pilot it. Too bad Alice had beaten her to it.

Turning, Iracebeth arched an eyebrow at the old

childhood ant farm she'd placed on a side table. An elaborate network of tunnels ran through the sand, and the creatures inside shuffled around busily.

"What do you think, my pets?" she asked, her voice oily.

She stepped over and with two fingers lifted a dome covering a nearby plate. On top of it rested a tiny white cake.

"Look," Iracebeth said, taunting them. "How close you are to your salvation! I'm talking to you." She bent down and tapped on the glass, jostling the sand.

When the tiresome beasts didn't move fast enough, Iracebeth picked up the whole ant farm and shook it. "Earthquake! Ha-ha!" She laughed shrilly.

From far away, she heard a screeching sound. Curious, Iracebeth set down the ant farm, oblivious to the now frantic movements of its occupants. The

Red Queen sauntered to the window and pulled back the curtain.

Up in the sky, a wooden and metal machine was squeaking toward her castle. As it neared, she recognized Time pumping hard at several levers. What was he doing?

The machine wobbled in the air, then dropped toward the very window where she stood.

Iracebeth leapt back as Time's contraption careened through the window.

Bang! The wooden platform smashed into the floor. A metal cog broke off and rolled away, bumping into a root near the wall. Time lay panting amid the rubble of his machine.

Picking her way over to him, Iracebeth frowned.

"Where the devil have you been?" she snapped. "Where is Alice? Where's my Chronosphere?"

"She's gone." Time gasped for breath, each word a struggle. "She took it!"

Chapter Fifteen

"What?" Iracebeth exploded. "You let her get away?" She needed that Chronosphere! It was the key to her revenge on Mirana.

Time reached out and used part of his ruined Tempus Fugit to climb to his feet.

"You don't understand," he said. He peeled back his vest and pointed anxiously at his heart clock. It was ticking slowly and softly, its face almost entirely obscured by rust.

"I must find her! Where is she?" Time asked.

"How should I know where she is?" Iracebeth said irritably. *He* was the one who'd lost her.

"She's your enemy! She—" Time broke off. "Hightopps!" he cried. "She kept talking about Hightopps! She says she knows where they are. She said she was going to rescue them. Do you know what that means?"

As Time looked at her with desperate hope, Iracebeth pursed her lips and turned to consider the room, her eyes resting on the ant farm. Several new tunnels had already been constructed. She smiled grimly, a plan clicking into place in her clever, oversized brain.

"I know exactly what it means," she said. She raised her voice. "Guards!"

Two giant soldiers, who were actually animated vegetables—the best Iracebeth could come up with, given her circumstances—lumbered into the room. Their pointed noses drooped and tufts of withered greens sprouted up from their heads through their helmets.

"Put him in the dungeon!" the Red Queen commanded, pointing imperiously at Time.

"What?" Time's jaw dropped. "Wait! My dearest, you can't! It will not work, it is impossible to stop Time!"

The soldiers grabbed his arms and wrestled him toward the door. Time's eyes rounded in surprise and he collapsed between them.

"Oh, it is possible. I see," he observed.

Iracebeth loomed above him, a wicked gleam in her eyes.

"From now on, *I'm* in charge," she declared.

Triumphant, the Red Queen led the way down the stairwell, her soldiers dutifully following her with their prisoner. Time had finally been caught.

Alice burst through the door into Hatter's house, too excited to bother knocking.

"Hatter!" she shouted. "Your family! They're alive!"

His main room was empty and he didn't emerge from the back. After a quick glance around, she ran up the bright blue spiral staircase to the second floor.

It opened directly into the bedroom, where she found her friends clustered around Hatter's bed. Hatter himself was stretched out on the mattress, his eyes closed, his once vibrantly orange hair now a limp white.

McTwisp was holding a stethoscope to Hatter's chest, but as Alice approached, he removed it and shook his head sadly. His nose quivered.

"The Forgettingfulness," Tweedledee said.

"It's unfilled his head," Tweedledum finished for him. The brothers rocked gently from side to side, unable to bear it.

"We fear you are too late," the White Queen said softly from her place by the bed.

Alice couldn't—wouldn't—believe that to be true. She hurried forward to sit on the edge of the bed, and took Hatter's hand. His skin was clammy and cool and his pulse was faint.

"You were right," she whispered fiercely. "They're alive!"

But Hatter didn't even twitch at her voice.

"I can't bear to see him like this!" Mallymkun sniffed.

Bayard gently nosed her to crawl onto his head

and carried her down the stairs, the rest of the group trudging after them. Mirana paused for one last wistful glance, but Hatter's face remained dead to the world. Slipping away, she left Alice alone with the comatose Hatter.

A patch of color caught Alice's eye and she turned to find the blue paper hat on Hatter's nightstand. Gently picking it up, she fingered the spiraling paper.

"I know what this means, Hatter," she said softly. "You made it for your father when you were young."

She looked up, but there was no change. Undeterred, she continued.

"And remember the magic tree, Hatter? It wasn't magic, it was him." Alice pictured Zanik sneaking out in the dark of night to leave candy for his son. "All those years, it was your father. And on the day the Jabberwocky attacked, he left the blue hat there as a message that they'd survived!"

At a flicker of movement beneath Hatter's eyelids, Alice sat forward eagerly.

"Because he kept it, Hatter," she said. Taking Hatter's hands in her own, she cupped them around the paper hat. "That blue hat you thought he threw away. All his life, a token of his love, his love for you, his son."

Hatter's body shivered slightly.

"And he still does, Hatter. Because he's alive!" Alice finished emphatically.

At her words, Hatter's eyes blinked open slowly. He gazed at the blue hat in his hands.

"He . . . kept it?" he asked tentatively.

"Yes!" Alice nearly shouted. She jumped up and grabbed Hatter's shoulders. "Yes, I was there. I saw it. He picked it up and kept it. Your family is *alive*!"

Hatter propped himself up on his elbows and peered at Alice, recognition dawning in his eyes.

Chapter Fifteen

"It is you, isn't it? I'd know you anywhere. You're Alice!" he said.

Bursting with joy, Alice flung her arms around him. "Oh, Hatter!" she cried. "I've missed you so much!"

Color crept back into Hatter's face and hair. He patted Alice's back as she hugged him. But when she leaned away, his gaze was sober.

"Why have they not come home?" he asked.

"Because they are being held captive," Alice explained. "By the only person cruel enough to keep them locked up all these years—"

"The bloody big head!" Hatter bolted upright, his head nearly brushing the canopy over his bed as he stood on the mattress. His eyes were bright with purpose, his shoulders set. He was the picture of vengefulness—besides the flowing nightgown he wore.

"I'm going to find the Red Queen," Hatter

proclaimed, grabbing Alice's hand and stepping down to the floor. "And bring my family home!"

Alice squeezed his hand. They would do it together.

Five minutes later, they strode out of Hatter's house. Hatter wore a safari outfit only he could pull off: a dark blue pith helmet, which matched his plaid pants; a plum riding jacket; and brown leather boots buckled up to his knees. He'd also insisted Alice change out of her dreadful asylum garb, so she was now cinched into a tailored black vest, a bright red blouse, puffy gray pantaloons, and laced-up boots.

With a high whistle, Alice summoned the Bandersnatch, and a few moments later, he bounded out of the woods. His broad mouth was open, displaying rows of pointed teeth, but he panted happily as he wriggled up to Alice. Hatter pulled out some riding equipment, and together they saddled the Bandersnatch. The white-haired beast shook his fur, the black spots along his body rippling as Alice and Hatter climbed aboard.

"Come on, we've got a family to save," Alice said. She turned the Bandersnatch down the path into Tulgey Woods and clucked her tongue.

The beast gathered his muscles and leapt forward. As they rode into a clearing, they found their friends gathered under a tree. Mirana's hands rested on the Tweedles' shoulders while Mallymkun viciously thrashed her needle-sword at blades of grass. The White Rabbit and the March Hare pawed sadly at their ears, and Bayard was sprawled out with his head on Mirana's foot, his eyes mournful.

"Hatter!" Mallymkun cried joyfully as the Bandersnatch clawed to a stop in the grass.

"He's altogether back in pieces," the Tweedles exclaimed together.

Hatter swept off his helmet and bowed, his orange hair almost aglow.

"The very same," Hatter said. "Now, if you will

excuse us, there are urgent matters of rescue and vengeance ahead."

Without hesitation, Bayard sprang up. "I cannot let you face this danger alone," he said. "You have my nose."

"And my sword," the Dormouse offered.

"And my brother," the Tweedles said, pointing at each other.

The White Queen smiled and stroked the Bandersnatch's nose fondly as she looked up at Hatter. "We are all coming with you."

XVI

A ROW OF GLACIERS bordered the Outlands. Alice shivered on the Bandersnatch and dug her hands deeper into his fur as the beast padded through a tunnel in the icy mountains.

On the other side, the Outlands themselves stretched for hundreds of miles. Jagged mountains pierced the skyline here and there, but nothing moved against the fields of rolling grass in between.

Not wanting to linger, Alice and Hatter spurred the Bandersnatch onward. Bayard bounded alongside them, Mallymkun riding at his collar. The

Tweedles and Thackery rumbled up next on a cart. Mirana rode atop a white steed, McTwisp clinging to her nervously. As they crossed the grasslands, Alice and her friends went over the plan again. The Red Queen must be holding the Hightopps captive somewhere in her Outlands castle, so once inside, they would split up to search every possible room.

At last Iracebeth's castle came into view. It was shaped like a giant heart and seemed woven entirely out of red vines. Gray storm clouds rolled ominously around its curves. Alice thought it a very bleak place indeed and felt a stab of pity for Iracebeth. She quickly shook it off. Even if she had once been a helpless little girl, the Red Queen was now a merciless, power-hungry tyrant.

"My family is there," Hatter said. "I know it."

Alice nodded; she could sense it, too. Somewhere within those walls, the Hightopps were being held prisoner.

They pulled up to the castle's entrance, which was unguarded. Alice looked around the main hall suspiciously. The walls—made of spongy plant matter—bulged slightly, and pillars of twisting vines held up the ceiling of the tall central chamber. Winding up from the floor, a stairwell composed entirely of roots and vines branched off in different directions. If it hadn't been for the bloodred coloring of all the plants, it might have been oddly beautiful. Instead, it almost seemed as though they were standing inside a heart, especially since the plants on the walls pulsated slightly.

The White Rabbit rubbed his paws over his nose and glanced around nervously. "Is this where we—"

"Split up!" Mallymkun called out excitedly.

The friends divided into groups and explored different hallways. Alice and Hatter walked elbow to elbow down a long corridor that ended in two doorways. As they approached, vines grew up over one of the passages, forcing them through the other into an upward stairwell. The steps creaked under their feet.

Alice paused next to an open doorway, hearing something tick inside. Poking her head in, she saw a large black grandfather clock wrapped in red vines.

"She has one, too," Alice said with a jolt. "That's how she visits Time!"

But Hatter wasn't there to hear. He had continued on, and now his figure disappeared around a turn. Not wanting to be separated, Alice hurried to catch up.

At the top of the stairs was a solid wooden door covered in carvings of hearts.

Lowering his shoulder, Hatter shoved the door open.

"Father! Mother! Anyone . . . ?" he called as he bounded inside, Alice on his heels.

The room had Iracebeth's stamp all over it. A series of cabbage, turnip, and carrot heads hung from chains, their faces frozen in cries of pain. Lining a set of shelves were bottles of poisonous plants, scorpions, and unidentifiable blobs Alice guessed were equally dangerous.

With a gasp, Alice noticed a skeleton, sporting a dunce's cap, propped in the bed. A heart-shaped eye patch over one of the skull's sockets identified it as having once belonged to Stayne, Iracebeth's former paramour and lackey. Alice recalled that as soon as the Red Queen had been deposed, Stayne had tried to kill her rather than be sentenced to permanent exile with her. Perhaps he had never truly loved Iracebeth. Either way, he had not survived her punishment.

Stifling a shudder, Alice glanced around the rest of the chamber. She spotted what looked like the remnants of Time's travel machine piled to one side. She wondered if Time was truly on Iracebeth's side. Did he really trust her? He must not know what had become of her last lover.

Hatter finished searching the room and turned to Alice in despair. "They're not here," he said. His knees buckling, he plopped down to the dirt floor. "I was certain they were here. I could *feel* it."

Kneeling next to him, Alice patted his shoulder gently. They would keep looking. The Hightopps had to be there somewhere.

Hatter sighed and looked up; then his eyes grew wide.

On a table sat an ant farm. The tunnels within were suddenly forming a shape—which looked to be the outline of a top hat.

Hatter leapt to his feet, picked up the ant farm, and brought his face right up to the glass. Tears pricked his eyes, but he smiled broadly.

Inside, several tiny people with bright red hair waved up at him, banging their hands against the glass.

"Father! Mother! Everyone!" Hatter cried happily. "It's you! Teeny tiny yous."

He leaned down and kissed the glass, just as—

Clang! A heavy grate of vines slammed down over the nearest window, interrupting the happy moment. Then: *Clang! Clang! Clang!* Grates fell to block off all the remaining windows.

Alice and Hatter spun to face the door.

There stood the smirking Red Queen. Behind her, four vegetable soldiers formed a tight guard.

"Hello, *Alice*," Iracebeth said acidly.

Two of the guards moved forward and grabbed Alice, patting her down.

"Thank you ever so much," Iracebeth continued in a sickly sweet tone. "You have delivered to me the most powerful device in the entire Universe."

The guards wrestled the Chronosphere away from Alice and handed it to Iracebeth.

"Along with the person whom I hold truly responsible." Iracebeth turned as more of her guards arrived in the hallway, escorting the White Queen.

Mirana's face appeared serene, but the prisoners behind her were less poised. The Tweedles clung to each other, and Bayard had his tail tucked between his legs. Thackery's eyes rolled side to side nervously, while McTwisp's teeth chattered. Mallymkun was, of course, the only one putting up a fight. A soldier held her far away from his side, even as her fists swung fiercely.

Iracebeth chuckled, clearly enjoying herself.

As he clutched the ant farm to his chest, Hatter eyed the Red Queen. "I recall now why I don't like her," he said.

"Now we shall see justice!" Iracebeth shouted. She followed her guards as they shoved their prisoners back down the stairwell—all except for Alice and Hatter.

Although Alice sprang after them, another grate crashed into the floor, blocking the doorway. She grabbed the bars, seeing Iracebeth cast her one last smug look before disappearing around a bend.

Hatter turned back to the ant farm, where his father stood at the top of the sand.

"Tarrant?" Zanik called in a small voice through the glass. "Is that really you? I'd stopped believing so long ago it feels impossible."

Smiling, Hatter replied, "It's not impossible, merely unpossible."

"Oh, Hatter," Alice cried from the door. She'd been trying to squeeze through the bars, but it was no use. "What have I done? We have to stop her! We have to get out of here."

Hatter looked at Alice, then at his family. Then he pulled out the blue paper hat he'd brought along for luck, his eyes alight with a crazy idea.

XVII

His brow furrowed in concern, Zanik peered up at his son. This was by far the scariest thing he had ever done. Stalling, he ran his hands along the blue paper airplane once more. His son had constructed it out of the blue paper hat, and it *seemed* sturdy enough—for a paper airplane.

Uneasy, Zanik stepped into the center of the airplane, testing its balance. Hatter cheerfully picked up the airplane, causing his father to topple over within it, and carried it to the window.

Whistling shrilly, the wind whipped past the

high tower. The ground seemed hundreds of miles away. Zanik brought his hand up to his head.

"I feel like I've traded the frying pan for the fire. This is crazy," he shouted.

"Someone once said wisdom is born from total insanity," Hatter said sagely.

"Who said that?" Zanik asked.

"Me, just now." Hatter pulled his arm back and then launched the paper airplane through the grated window before his father could protest.

"Aaaahhhhhhh!" Zanik screamed as the airplane zoomed through the air.

Only, now that he was flying, it wasn't quite as scary anymore. Zanik shifted in his seat, redirecting the plane. It whirled in a loop, tipping Zanik upside down for a moment.

Zanik screamed once more, this time in excitement.

The plane coasted down and landed in a patch of grass. Zanik stood up and stepped out lightly, patting the blue paper affectionately, his mouth stretched in a grin.

Thunk! A paw shook the ground, and the meager sunlight overhead disappeared. Something wet hit Zanik's hat.

He slowly raised his eyes.

A white beast loomed above him, a stream of saliva dripping from his razor-sharp teeth.

Zanik gulped, then straightened and addressed the animal his son had assured him was on their side. "Good day to you," he said. "My name is Zanik Hightopp. I wondered if you might give me a hand releasing my family from their prison. It is rather an urgent matter."

Lowering his snout, the Bandersnatch sniffed Zanik loudly. Then he scuffed his front foot against the dirt and nodded. Relieved, Zanik scrambled up the beast's nose and hauled himself up onto his massive head. He settled right behind an ear, grabbing on to tufts of fur.

With a ferocious growl, the Bandersnatch reared up and turned toward the castle. As Zanik held on tight, the beast galloped into it and past all the grasping vines to the topmost tower.

Once they heard the Bandersnatch thumping up the stairs, Alice and Hatter rushed to the door, but they stepped back as the creature snapped his powerful jaws around the gate. In one move, the Bandersnatch yanked it away. He panted proudly as Alice rubbed his cheek and Hatter lifted Zanik off his back, then set him down next to the other Hightopps.

"Now to grow you back," Hatter said. He spotted the dome-covered plate on the table and removed the cover to reveal the Upelkuchen cake. "Aha."

Hatter broke off a piece of cake and gave it to Zanik.

"Not too much now," Hatter cautioned. "Careful."

Zanik nibbled at the cake, then passed it along to his family. Alice gathered blankets and sheets from around the room so they could fashion new clothes for themselves after they grew. In next to no time, the Hightopps were back to their regular heights, laughing and hugging one another.

Hatter set his shoulders as his father approached him.

"I see you haven't changed a bit," Zanik said, glancing at Hatter's zany attire.

"Nope." Hatter smiled, a nervous but determined gleam in his eye.

Zanik studied his son. "Good," he finally said.

Tears stinging his eyes, Hatter reached forward to hug his father. Just then, a shudder ran through the room, and Hatter's arms moved as though they were immersed in water. Alice spun—or she tried to. She, too, felt her body slow down as though it were trapped in honey.

Hatter's arms finally closed around his father with a thud as time returned to its regular speed. Confused, Hatter and Zanik stepped back and looked around.

"What the dickens was that?" Zanik asked.

Patches of rust had sprouted along cracks in the walls and floor. Alice touched one of the spots, her finger coming away covered in metallic red dust. It was the same powder she'd seen on Time's heart clock in Witzend when he'd begged her for the Chronosphere. It was *rust*. What if the Grand Clock was affected, too? Perhaps without the Chronosphere, it was losing power. . . . All signs seemed to point to the possibility that Time was grinding to a halt.

"Time! He's slowing down!" Alice exclaimed. "He's going to *stop*! I saw it. It's why he wanted the Chronosphere."

"Hang on," Hatter said. "If Time ends, we all end. He told me so himself."

Guilt swamped Alice. Because of her, the world might end. "This is my fault! I stole the Chronosphere. I should've been more careful with Time. I should have listened to him."

Hatter set his hands on her shoulders, forcing her to meet his eyes. Alice felt his confidence in her filling her with strength.

"We've got to stop the big head!" Hatter said fiercely.

"And get back the Chronosphere," Alice added.

The Bandersnatch smacked his lips loudly as though in agreement.

After surveying the discarded pieces of Time's vehicle lying on the floor, Alice turned to Hatter's family. "Hightopps!" she called. "Gather the pieces of his time machine. We may have need of it yet."

XVIII

The Red Queen's castle was eerily silent as Alice and Hatter crept down the stairs and into the main hall. Not even the leaves on the walls rustled.

"Where is everyone?" Alice whispered.

"Look!" Hatter pointed through a doorway to the garden, where what looked like an impromptu courtroom had been set up.

In the center of the grass, Mirana stood tall and dignified, with a determined McTwisp at her side. Bordering the courtyard was a line of

vegetable soldiers, including several who guarded the Tweedles, Thackery, Bayard, and Mallymkun. Before them all, on a raised platform, Iracebeth gleefully bounced on her toes in front of a throne of branches. Time was chained to a smaller, less decorated throne set next to Iracebeth's. His face was haggard and he was clutching his heart. In her typical self-involved way, Iracebeth appeared oblivious to the fact that she was killing Time.

"We're too late," Alice said, taking in Time's condition.

"He's almost out of himself. We must hurry." Hatter took her hand and squeezed it. They couldn't give up yet.

"Mirana of Marmoreal!" Iracebeth declared loudly, glaring down at her sister. "You are accused of treason. I hereby sentence you to—"

"Wait!" McTwisp objected. "What about the verdict?"

Chapter Eighteen

"Sentence first! Then verdict," Iracebeth bellowed. Her gaze snapped back to Mirana. "You are banished to the Outlands," Iracebeth continued. Her voice was now almost hushed, and it trembled slightly. "No one is to show you kindness or ever speak a word to you. You will not have a friend in the world."

Mirana faced her sister, her eyes wide.

Taking a deep breath, Iracebeth lifted her chin defiantly. "You have lied. You have stolen. You are *not* the rightful queen of Underland," she said.

The White Rabbit bounded forward. "Objection! Where's your proof?"

"I don't need proof," Iracebeth spat. "I've got better. I shall have a confession!" She lifted the Chronosphere, its metal bands glinting brightly.

Puzzled, Mirana drew her eyebrows together as Iracebeth descended toward her. The Red Queen threw the Chronosphere to the ground and it immediately expanded to its traveling-through-time size. As the bands spun and whirred, the lights along its edges glowed white. A jolt ran through Alice as she realized Iracebeth's plan.

"Wait!" Alice burst from hiding. "Stop! Wait!"

Everyone turned to stare at her as she rushed across the courtyard.

"You cannot change the past, Your Majesty," Alice cried. "Believe me, I have tried."

Narrowing her eyes, Iracebeth huffed angrily—of course Alice would try to protect Mirana. But Iracebeth would have justice! Before anyone could stop her, she latched on to her sister's arm and tugged her past the whizzing bands into the heart of the Chronosphere.

Both Alice and Hatter raced forward, but it was too late. Iracebeth expertly steered the Chronosphere into the sky. Alice stared upward, watching the golden ball wink against the clouds before it disappeared completely.

Frantic, Alice spun to face the crowd. "We've got to stop her!" she cried.

Unfortunately, it was the vegetable soldiers who lurched into motion. They lowered their spears and advanced on Alice and Hatter.

With a tremendous roar, the Bandersnatch leapt into the courtyard, the Hightopps on his back. The soldiers scattered left and right, terrified to their roots by the snarling beast, who growled happily as they fled.

Clambering up on the stage, Alice and Hatter rushed to Time. The rust had spread across his body and he was slumped to the side.

"You've got to take us back," Alice told Time as she and Hatter untied him. "She's going to change the past!"

Time gazed blankly at Alice and then at the grass, where Zanik and the rest of the Hightopps were laying out the pieces of the Tempus Fugit. His eyes clouded over, his face weary.

"I let my heart distract me from the schedule." His voice was filled with remorse. "I'm a disgrace to the profession, the concept, myself."

His chin dropped to his chest and he let out a deep sigh.

"C'mon, old chap," Hatter said. "Don't give yourself a hard time."

But Time just shook his head slowly. "I'm too weak," he wheezed.

"No, you're not." Alice poked his shoulder. "You're Time. The Infinite . . ."

"The Immortal!" Hatter cried.

"I'm beginning to wonder about that last part," Time muttered.

"And besides," Hatter continued, ignoring him, "you're the only person who can rebuild that thing." He pointed to the array of cogs, chains, wooden levers, and beams that were spread out like a jigsaw puzzle before them.

As Time's eyes finally focused on the pieces,

a spark lit deep within him. It was his nature to march onward! After casting a quick smile at Hatter and Alice, he shuffled toward the parts. It was about time he got to work.

Just a few ticks later—longer, admittedly, than it had taken the first time—the Tempus Fugit was ready. Time gave it one final inspection, then nodded to Alice and Hatter.

The three of them climbed aboard and began pumping the levers to launch it skyward. Everyone else gathered to wish them good luck, waving as the Tempus Fugit vanished.

Pulling at the machine's levers with all her might, Alice glanced overboard. The Ocean of Time flickered below, various moments bubbling to the surface.

There was a stunned Hatter beside the trunk of a tree, carefully lifting the rumpled blue paper hat and staring at it, dumbstruck.

Next Alice herself appeared, battling the

Jabberwocky during her last trip to Underland. On the Tempus Fugit, Alice felt a weird combination of nausea and pride, remembering that day.

A tea party swam into view, but it wasn't one Alice had attended. Time sat impatiently at the table as Hatter cavorted around him. Warmth filled Alice's chest as she realized the Hatter below was delaying Time for her! And that was no easy task. Some might say impossible, but those someones didn't know Hatter *or* Alice.

Time also gazed below, but he saw something troubling. Every day was tinged with a smattering of reddish brown. Noticing his somber expression, Alice took a second look and her confidence sank.

The rust was spreading. They didn't have much time.

XIX

HATTER LEANED forward like the prow of a ship as they cut their way deeper into the past. His eagle eyes spotted a flicker of movement ahead.

"There they are! Hurry!" he cried.

Alice, Hatter, and Time flung themselves at the pumps and levers, eking out more speed from the Tempus Fugit.

As the Chronosphere's golden light bobbed closer, they could see the royal sisters within its spinning rings. Mirana's face was pale and drawn,

and she eyed Iracebeth warily. Ignoring her sister, Iracebeth had her eyes locked on the ocean. Her tongue peeked out from one side of her mouth, like that of a cat that's cornered a mouse.

Then Iracebeth yanked on a lever and the Chronosphere dove toward a specific day in the past. She steered the Chronosphere through a chilly gray sky. The town of Witzend appeared below, windows glowing as people lit lanterns and fires indoors.

The Chronosphere squeezed through an opening in Witzend Castle and rolled to a stop in an abandoned corridor. New spiderwebs of rust traced down the stone walls and along the floor, but Iracebeth, intent on her goal, didn't notice. Her fingers clutched her sister's arm, and she pulled her from the Chronosphere, which began to shrink into a tiny ball.

"Where are we?" Mirana asked.

"You know where we are," Iracebeth answered darkly.

Chapter Nineteen

As Mirana looked around, she realized she *did* know: they were just outside their childhood bedroom. And she had a pretty good guess as to *when* they were. Her forehead creased and she hung back as Iracebeth cracked open the door.

Queen Elsmere's voice rang out from the room. "Why are these crusts under your bed?" Mirana's shoulders stiffened.

"She put them there!" Iracebeth's young voice cried out.

"Did you, Mirana?" Elsmere asked.

In the hallway, the older Iracebeth rounded on her sister. "Did you, Mirana?" she whispered accusingly.

From within the room, they could hear the younger Iracebeth becoming insistent. "You did! Tell her!"

"Tell the truth, Mirana," Queen Elsmere commanded sternly. "Did you eat the tarts and put the crusts there?"

The sisters both tensed; they knew what came next. Iracebeth's face flushed with anger, and Mirana's eyes were full of regret.

Bang! Alice, Hatter, and Time crashed into the corridor. Startled, the queens jumped, but Iracebeth quickly tugged her sister toward their bedroom door. She didn't want Mirana to squirm away; this was what she had brought her there to see. This was the moment that proved it was all Mirana's fault. At last, Mirana would have to tell their mother the truth and the past would be righted.

"No," Mirana's younger self whispered.

Gong! The clock tower in Witzend sang out, its toll carrying far through the wintry air. Scooping up the Chronosphere from the stone hallway, Alice hurried toward the queens, with Time and Hatter at her side.

Years of betrayal, loneliness, and anger roared up in Iracebeth as she heard her sister deny the crime again, and she reached for the door, ready to fling it open.

"Iracebeth, wait!" Mirana cried, grabbing her sister's arm. "I . . . I lied."

Iracebeth blinked, taken aback.

"I ate the tarts," Mirana continued. "And I lied about it." Tears welled in her deep brown eyes. "If I had just told the truth, none of this would have ever happened. I'm so sorry."

Alice and the others came to a halt a few feet away, caught up in the intensity of the moment.

"Forgive me. Please. If you can," Mirana finished.

Looking into Mirana's face, Iracebeth remembered when they used to be the best of friends.

They would giggle together as they played hopscotch. At the beach, they had made the most amazing pink sand castle together. It had four tall crooked towers circling the main one. Hand in hand, Mirana and Iracebeth had combed the beach to find the prettiest shells to decorate it. Iracebeth hadn't wanted to go back home that day. The sun had been bright in the sky, and the breeze from the ocean had been just enough to keep them cool on the sand. There had even been happy music emanating from a nearby lobster quadrille.

Sometimes at night, the girls had curled up together to read. There had been an incredibly comfy window bench, and they had spent hours there, caught up in a story about a lion or a unicorn. Iracebeth had waited patiently for Mirana—the slower reader—to reach the end of the page before she turned to the next. Iracebeth's hair, always more stubborn than Mirana's, would fall into her eyes and Mirana would gently tuck it back behind her ears for her.

Iracebeth felt a tear slide down her cheek at the memories.

"That's all I ever wanted to hear. Really it was," she said, sniffing.

Chapter Nineteen

Overcome with emotion, Mirana and Iracebeth collapsed into each other's arms. For the first time in many years, Iracebeth felt warm from the inside out.

Creak. The bedroom door opened fully. The younger Iracebeth ran out, and she crashed into Mirana's and Iracebeth's skirts and stumbled backward.

"Oh, bother," Iracebeth the older said.

The child version of her looked directly into her older self's oversized face. She paused in shock. Then she screamed and screamed until—

Poof!

Both Iracebeths froze, an orangey-red powder crusting over their skin.

"Iracebeth!" Mirana cried.

Like a firework going off, rust exploded from the two Iracebeths, then crawled along the carpet and up Elsmere and the younger Mirana until they, too, were statues.

But the rust didn't stop there.

It kept spreading, corroding everything around them.

"Oh, this can't be good," Hatter mumbled.

"She has broken the past! We've got to get to the Grand Clock before it stops forever," Time cried.

The Grand Clock was not faring well. Wilkins frowned as he and the Seconds pumped levers and greased cogs.

"Come on, chaps! Keep it swinging," Wilkins called, his voice desperate. He looked around in dismay.

Rust was spreading throughout the Grand Clock, making the gears grind slower and throwing off the delicate balance of the clockwork.

The Seconds began to slow down, tiring. Wilkins knew they were running out of themselves. Where could Time be?

Chapter Nineteen

Time was hunched inside the Chronosphere, holding his side in pain as Alice and the rest of their group crowded in next to him. Shooting Time a worried look, Alice steered the Chronosphere out of Witzend Castle and up into the snowy sky. Below them, a circle of rust rippled out from the castle, carpeting the streets, painting the buildings red, and halting people and animals mid-breath.

Gon—

The chime of the church's clock cut off abruptly as rust covered the tower.

Even the snowflakes froze in midair, the white specks turning into muddy dots of red and brown.

Hatter's mouth tugged down at the sight.

"I still don't understand why we had to bring *her* with us," he muttered to Alice. He glanced at the rust-frozen figure stretched out on the bottom of the Chronosphere, taking up most of the floor space. Mirana had tears running down her cheeks as she cradled Iracebeth's head in her lap. But

Hatter couldn't summon much sympathy for the Red Queen.

Alice patted his shoulder with her free hand. She knew how hard it could be to forgive. But she was discovering that everyone had a past. Nobody was *all* good or *all* bad. Iracebeth had had her share of pain; she just hadn't known how to handle it.

The Chronosphere popped out into the flowing light above the Ocean of Time, and Alice spun them toward the present.

Yet a troubling new wave had formed in the ocean below them. Like a row of toy soldiers falling down, one after another, the days began to crackle, each one's moments infiltrated by rust.

"It's catching up!" Hatter cried worriedly.

Sparing a glance over her shoulder, Alice saw the rust sweeping toward them. She gritted her teeth and tugged on a chain, demanding more speed from the Chronosphere. *Come on, come on,* she urged silently.

They rocketed forward, flashing by familiar days. But the rust was right behind them, invading the scenes of their past. Finally, they burst into the present above Iracebeth's castle.

The Hightopps and Alice's friends stared up as the Chronosphere zoomed by.

"That crazy boy might actually pull this off—" Zanik was saying when a wave of rust slammed into him, freezing him with his mouth open.

The rust swept over the others, catching Bayard, McTwisp, Mallymkun, and Thackery. The Tweedles backed up as far as they could, huddling together, but the wave washed over them, as well.

As Hatter saw his family and friends suspended mid-motion, their eyes wide with alarm, he winced.

"Hurry, Alice, please," Hatter urged.

Alice threw her weight against a lever, and the Chronosphere banged inside Iracebeth's castle. Ricocheting off a column of vines, it rolled along a corridor. Leaves and roots peeled off the walls as metallic fragments weighed them down, and the ceiling began to crumble in patches.

Behind them, the doors to the castle burst open, and a liquid wave of rust poured into the chamber. It splashed against the wall and split into two waves that bore down on the Chronosphere while Alice maneuvered it up the root staircase.

With a loud creak, a section of ceiling gave way and crashed into the space where the Chronosphere had just been. Time groaned as he gazed through the new gap: the sky had turned a gritty red and brown as rust cascaded down on the land.

Doing her best to concentrate, Alice tugged on a lever, and the Chronosphere pivoted, spinning into a room off the stairwell. Ahead of them, Iracebeth's black grandfather clock loomed.

Two waves of rust flooded into the room, racing along the curved walls toward the clock. Eyeing the distance and the waves, Hatter didn't think they would make it.

Chapter Nineteen

"Well, I've really enjoyed our time together, Alice," Hatter said. A wistful smile crossed his face.

Alice ignored him. She, too, was making calculations. Without warning, she slammed on the brakes, sending the Chronosphere into a tight spin. As it whirled in place, the two waves crashed into each other in front of the clock. Then they both receded for a moment, the force of their impact reversing their directions.

Seeing their chance, Alice threw off the brakes and thrust the Chronosphere forward, straight toward the clock.

Boom! The clock exploded as the Chronosphere crashed through it and plummeted into the dark space beyond, rust pouring through the gap behind it.

Alice spotted Time's castle in the distance and coaxed more speed from the Chronosphere. *Almost there,* she thought. She aimed for a stained glass window, and with a *crash, bang, boom*, the Chronosphere smashed through it and bounced along the floor of the Grand Clock's chamber.

Finally knocking into a pillar, the Chronosphere spun to a stop, spitting everyone out, as though it couldn't handle holding them any longer. Time went flying and Iracebeth's metal frame clanked against the floor. Alice staggered to her feet and snatched up the shrinking Chronosphere. With no time to waste, she raced along the floor toward the center of the Grand Clock, her friends just behind her. Close on their heels, waves of liquid rust crashed into the room from all sides, pouring toward the Grand Clock.

Alice led the charge, with Time, Hatter, and Mirana running behind her, dodging around unrecognizable stalagmites and lumps. With a grimace, Alice realized some of them were the struggling, rust-decayed forms of Seconds, Minutes, and Hours. Closer to the center, they passed by Wilkins, his body cemented to the ground with rust.

"We did our best, sir," Wilkins said as Time drew near.

Time saluted him but kept running. Now waves of rust lapped at the group's feet. Mirana fell first; then Wilkins was washed over. Encircling Hatter's legs, the rust began to climb upward.

"Alice," Hatter said, his voice carrying a mixture of sadness and hope.

Alice wouldn't stop, *couldn't* stop. Everything depended on her.

She hopped through the Grand Clock, whose pieces were barely moving now. The gears were almost stationary and the hammers creaked up and down at a snail's pace.

A few steps behind her, Time cried out as the wave of rust caught up to him. He sank to his knees, then crumpled under its weight.

It was the end of Time.

The hammer above Alice froze as the Grand

Clock gave out. Stepping into the gap at the center of the clock, Alice felt something wrap around her ankles. The odd sensation moved up her legs, encasing her in a gritty metal powder.

As her waist became constricted, she stretched up, focusing her eyes on the center of the clock.

Rust raced up her outstretched arm. With one final push, her fingers slammed the Chronosphere into place, then froze a hairsbreadth away.

Underland lay silent and motionless under a blanket of rust.

Not a puff of breath or a beating heart could be heard.

There could be no world without Time.

XX

N EERIE STILLNESS hung in the Chamber of the Grand Clock. Then . . .

tick

tock

Tick

Tock

Ticktock.

TICKTOCK.

Glowing under a layer of rust, like a cloth-covered lantern, the Chronosphere hummed to life, and the Grand Clock started up. Rust flaked off the machinery as cogs wheeled and barrels lifted.

The tip of Alice's finger turned from red to pink as the rust moved backward, washed away by the restoration of time. Slowly, Alice returned to herself. After taking in a gulp of air, she looked around. Had she done it? Had she fixed Time?

Time coughed as the rust melted off him. Beyond him, she could see Wilkins, Seconds, Minutes, and Hours wriggling to life.

Alice picked her way over to Time, who was now sitting up. "Are you all right?" she asked.

He looked slightly dazed, but his eyes lifted in gratitude to meet hers and he nodded before conducting a self-inspection, patting himself down and checking his heart clock. His head cocked at an angle, he listened carefully for the slightest hiccup.

Alice stepped away to find her friends. As the coppery red wave receded across the chamber, it liberated everyone. When their eyesight cleared, Mirana and Iracebeth spotted each other, and Mirana rushed to her sister.

"Can you ever forgive me, Racie?" she asked.

With pursed lips, Iracebeth studied her.

"I can," she said. The words seemed to surprise even her. "I can!" she repeated happily. The sisters embraced, smiles stretching across their faces.

There was a clattering of many footsteps in the hall, and then a large group tumbled into the room. Zanik strode in at the front of the rest of the Hightopps, Bayard close behind, the Dormouse on his back. McTwisp and Thackery hopped along after them, and last, but not least, the Tweedles waddled in.

"Tarrant!" Zanik called out loudly, his face eager.

Hatter whirled. "Father!" he cried, running toward him. "This whole time, I thought you were—but you weren't—and you couldn't come see me because you were—and you kept the hat!" Hatter tripped over his words as he hugged his father tightly.

"Of course I kept it," Zanik said. "It was a gift

from you. But the greatest gift we have is the time we have together. And I promise, I'll never waste another second." He stepped back, his hands resting on Hatter's shoulders. "We have a lot of catching up to do," he continued.

"I make hats, Father! I'm a hatter!" Hatter exclaimed proudly.

Tears pricked Zanik's eyes. "I want to see every one, Tarrant," he said in a choked voice. "I want to see every hat you've ever made."

"I promise," Hatter said as Zanik pulled him into another hug.

Elsewhere in the chamber, the Tweedles were also hugging.

"Let's never fight again," Tweedledum said.

"Were we fighting before?" Tweedledee asked. He stared at his brother in puzzlement.

"No, so why start now?" Tweedledum said.

Gazing across the room, Alice watched her

friends reunite with their families. Everyone seemed so happy, all their former fights—big and small—swept away. With a pang, she thought of her mother, wishing she were there to hold her close. The world had nearly ended, and Alice and her mother had not parted on good terms.

Time walked over to Alice. Sure he was going to scold her, she hung her head. The whole mess *was* her fault.

Time seemed to read her mind and laid a hand gently on her shoulder.

"All that is really worth doing is what we do for others," he said simply.

Alice looked up at him, her eyes full of regret. "I owe you an apology," she said. "You tried to warn me about the Chronosphere, but I didn't listen."

"No worries, my dear." Time winked at her. "I heal all wounds."

Alice smiled. "You know," she said. "I used to

think you were a thief, stealing everything I loved. But you give before you take. And every day is a gift. Every hour, every minute, every second."

Reaching into her pocket, she pulled out her father's broken pocket watch. She ran her finger over the case one last time and then handed it to Time.

"Ah, the fallen soldier," Time said as he took it. "I suppose you want me to fix it." His eyebrow twitched up at her.

"No," Alice answered. "I want you to have it."

Time blinked in shock. Nobody ever gave *him* presents. He glanced from the watch to Alice. "You said it was your father's," he said in surprise.

"It was my father's, but it's not my father." Alice's eyes wandered to the happy families around the room. It was important to spend time with the loved ones you had. "I've been holding on too tightly to all the wrong things," she said. She turned back to Time with a determined smile.

Chapter Twenty

Time regarded the pocket watch again; then he waved his hand in the air above it.

Tick, tick, tick, beat the little watch.

With gentle hands, Time lovingly tucked it into his breast pocket. Emotion lit his eyes as they met Alice's. "My dear girl," he said. "They say I am a friend to no man. But I shall remember you. Always."

Time bowed his head in farewell and then walked to Wilkins and the Seconds, who were gathered by the Grand Clock. Eager to have their leader back, Time's measures crowded around him.

Alice felt someone take her hand and she turned to see Hatter's beaming face.

"Come, Alice," he said. "You must meet my family, you'll love them. We're going to have so much fun together!" He bounced slightly on his toes, giddy with excitement.

But Alice just smiled wistfully at him. Her heart was tugging her elsewhere. Back in London, her mother needed her.

Seeing the sadness in her eyes, Hatter cocked his head, his expression turning more serious.

"Oh, but I'm forgetting you have a family of your own, don't you?" he said.

Alice nodded. Hatter gazed around the room. Mirana and Iracebeth spoke animatedly, their hands waving in the air. The Tweedles shuffled along together, watching the Seconds tick past. Hatter's own family members were standing nearby, waiting for him.

"Very important thing, a family," Hatter continued. "You only get the one."

Alice's mouth wobbled. "Hatter, I think it's time for me to go home," she said.

"I won't see you for tea tomorrow, will I?" he asked, smiling softly.

"I don't think so." Alice flung her arms around his neck, a few tears sliding down her face.

"Don't worry, Alice." Hatter patted her shoulder.

"In the palace of dreams we shall meet, and laugh, and play all our lives."

Alice stepped back to gaze up at him. "But a dream is not reality," she said.

Hatter took both her hands in his and leaned in close.

"Ah, but who's to say which is which?" Hatter winked.

Alice smiled, happy to have restored Hatter to himself, but sad that she would havc to leave Underland. She was going to miss it and him—all over again.

XXI

THE LIBRARY in the Ascot mansion was usually quite cozy, but Helen Kingsleigh shivered in her seat at the wide oak table. Next to her, Lady Ascot sent her a pitying look, but Helen didn't notice; her eyes were fixed on the two men across from her.

Hamish was tapping his fingers impatiently while James, his clerk, shuffled slowly through a stack of papers. Reading over one page, James would shake his head as though it wasn't what he was looking for, place it at the back of the pile, and then start the process over again.

Alexandra, also at the table, picked invisible lint off her dress, clearly bored. She hemmed significantly at her husband.

After glancing at her, Hamish shot James another annoyed glare, then coughed and turned to Helen.

"In the end, it's about what Alice needs, Mrs. Kingsleigh," Hamish said. His voice was as oily as his skin. "Whether she ever returns or not—"

"*When* she returns," Helen interrupted. She would never give up hope.

"Quite, my dear, quite," Lady Ascot said soothingly. She patted Helen's arm.

"Now, please, the ship's deeds—just sign here," Hamish said, waving his hand toward the papers James held.

Helen sighed and picked up the pen Hamish had laid in front of her.

However, instead of handing them over, James

just stared down at the papers as though time stood still.

"Mr. Harcourt, please," Hamish snapped. "Time is money!"

Reluctantly, the clerk placed the deed in front of Helen just as a new voice rang out:

"I'm afraid he most certainly is not!"

Everyone's heads whipped around to see Alice standing in the doorway. She strode forward confidently.

"Time is many things," she continued. "But he isn't money, Hamish, or our enemy, Mother." She nodded at each of them. "But he is real and we must take account of him, Mr. Harcourt, if we are to spend the days he grants us wisely—"

Helen dropped the pen as Alice reached her side.

"—and with those we love most," Alice finished, taking her mother's hands in her own.

Flustered, Hamish widened his eyes. "Where did you come from?" he asked Alice.

"I walked right through the walls," Alice said mischievously. *"Poof!"* She flicked her fingers at him.

As Hamish jumped back, his chair squeaked against the floorboards. James quickly hid a snicker of amusement behind his hand.

"I may not be able to change the past, but I can learn from it." Alice gazed down at Helen. "Sign the papers, Mother," she added calmly.

"You . . . *want* me to sign them?" Helen asked in confusion.

Nodding, Alice picked up the pen and handed it to her mother.

"But what about your dreams?" Helen asked, pressing her.

Alice shook her head slightly. "I used to think the *Wonder* meant everything, but it's just a ship. There is always another ship. But you and your well-being mean everything to me." Alice squeezed her mother's shoulder gently. "You're my mother, and I only get one."

Helen and Alice smiled at each other, their eyes full of love and forgiveness.

Feeling the need to reassert himself, Hamish cleared his throat, interrupting their moment.

"So, you've decided to be a clerk?" he asked Alice. He turned to his own mother without waiting for an answer. "She decided to become a clerk. I knew she'd give in." His mouth twisted in a smug sneer.

"You're not a nice man, Hamish," Helen said unexpectedly. She glared at him fiercely. "I'm glad my daughter didn't marry you."

Alice's face broke into a grin as Hamish pulled back, stung, and Alexandra let out a startled gasp.

Helen rose to her feet and lifted her chin proudly. "Alice can do whatever Alice chooses to do," she said. "And so can I!"

Linking arms, Helen and Alice swept from the room, heads held high. The Ascots could do nothing but stare after them, their mouths agape.

Some Time Later

Alice hunched over a worn desk, carefully making notes in a ledger. Behind her, a wall held cubbyholes filled with samples of different silks. The door across from her opened and James entered, holding up a marine chronometer.

Alice nodded and began patting her pockets.

"Here you go, ma'am," James said. Leaning forward, he offered her his own watch.

Alice smiled up at him as she took it and the chronometer, then carefully wound them to match.

"Perfect," she declared.

Alice shut the ledger and headed for the door, avoiding the enormous Chinese vases in the room. James followed her out to a busy wharf overlooking the Hong Kong harbor. The water glistened in the sun, and ships of all shapes and sizes swayed with the tide. Alice inhaled deeply, the salty tang of the ocean air lifting her spirits even higher.

She turned to see two men attaching a new sign above the building she'd just left. Even though she'd seen the sign before, the words on it still sent a thrill through her.

KINGSLEIGH & KINGSLEIGH TRADING CO.

"A full cargo aboard," James said as he stepped up to her side. "Do we commence with Kingsleigh and Kingsleigh's maiden voyage?"

"Best check with the commodore," Alice answered.

They wove through the crowd on the pier until they found the commodore, who was gazing out at the sea.

"Commodore, shall we head out of harbor?" James asked politely.

Smiling, Helen Kingsleigh turned to answer him. "Time and tide wait for no man, Mr. Harcourt," she replied cheerfully. Her face was tan and she was *not* wearing a corset.

"Or, indeed, woman," Alice added.

Alice led the way up the gangplank of the *Wonder*, her mother and friend at her back.

"Captain aboard!" James called to the crew. "Full sail, lads! Full sail!"

As the boatswain guided the *Wonder* out of the harbor and past a fleet of ships, Alice and her mother walked along the port side, taking in the view.

Alice leaned over the edge of the deck to watch as a royal Indian barge floated by, its scarlet and gold sails shimmering.

In the center of the barge, a tall Indian prince, dressed in pure white pants and an embroidered red tunic, sat cross-legged on a pile of cushions. He was pouring a glass of wine for his companion—none other than Alice's aunt Imogene!

Chapter Twenty-One

"I'm sorry I was so late," the prince was saying.

Aunt Imogene waved her hand and took the glass. "Don't worry, my dear," she said. "I always knew you'd come."

Alice laughed, the wind rustling her hair. With a wave to her aunt, she turned back to her ship. Taking her place at the wheel, Alice carefully hung first the chronometer and then James's watch in front of her, smiling at the comforting *tick-tick-tick* of the watch's second hand.

She would never take time for granted again, and she meant to savor every minute of it.

Alice placed her hands on the wheel and swung the *Wonder* into the harbor, ready for her next adventure. Only time would tell what the future held, but she couldn't wait to find out.

THE END